"I guess you have to decide which hand you'd rather die by."

Then she *smiled* as if that made any sense.

Nate had been perfecting his acting skills for years now, but they were failing him. So he had to rely on military stoicism. He had to wrap himself in the stillness of a navy SEAL.

It might be the only way to survive this.

"You probably need some time to think this over. That's okay," she said gently.

But the world didn't always afford a man time to think things over, to act. To make the right decisions. Would he be here if he'd had time to think back in that Middle Eastern town, where trust hadn't been thick on the ground? Between anyone.

No matter how gentle someone was, sometimes a man had to make a choice. Best as he could.

"We'll build up to it. Rush in too fast, too many people will wonder, question, speculate. They'll pay too much attention to it."

"I'm afraid we don't have that kind of time," Elsie said. "Not with a hit man on the way."

COWBOY
IN THE
CROSSHAIRS

—

NICOLE HELM

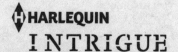

HARLEQUIN
INTRIGUE

For everyone who loved Blue Valley and followed me here.

Recycling programs
for this product may
not exist in your area.

ISBN-13: 978-1-335-48933-3

Cowboy in the Crosshairs

Copyright © 2021 by Nicole Helm

This edition published by arrangement with Harlequin Books S.A.

For questions and comments about the quality of this book,
please contact us at CustomerService@Harlequin.com.

Harlequin Enterprises ULC
22 Adelaide St. West, 41st Floor
Toronto, Ontario M5H 4E3, Canada
www.Harlequin.com

Printed in U.S.A.

Nicole Helm grew up with her nose in a book and the dream of one day becoming a writer. Luckily, after a few failed career choices, she gets to follow that dream—writing down-to-earth contemporary romance and romantic suspense. From farmers to cowboys, Midwest to *the* West, Nicole writes stories about people finding themselves and finding love in the process. She lives in Missouri with her husband and two sons and dreams of someday owning a barn.

Books by Nicole Helm

Harlequin Intrigue

A North Star Novel Series

Summer Stalker
Shot Through the Heart
Mountainside Murder
Cowboy in the Crosshairs

A Badlands Cops Novel

South Dakota Showdown
Covert Complication
Backcountry Escape
Isolated Threat
Badlands Beware
Close Range Christmas

Carsons & Delaneys: Battle Tested

Wyoming Cowboy Marine
Wyoming Cowboy Sniper
Wyoming Cowboy Ranger
Wyoming Cowboy Bodyguard

Visit the Author Profile page at Harlequin.com.

CAST OF CHARACTERS

Elsie Rogers—Head of IT for the secretive North Star group, Elsie must act as field operative when North Star's next mission involves her hometown.

Nathan (Nate) Averly—Former navy SEAL living at a rehabilitation ranch for soldiers who were injured or suffered PTSD. Everyone thinks Nate's suffering from paranoia due to his PTSD, but Nate is determined to get to the bottom of his dishonorable discharge.

Garrett Averly—Nate's brother. Blue Valley, Montana's sheriff. Worried about Nate's frame of mind.

Shay—Head of North Star, close friends with Elsie. She's in charge of sending Elsie into the field.

Connor Lindstrom—Former navy SEAL who served with Nate and was discharged at the same time. Nate sent Connor evidence of some shady dealings in the military, but it was destroyed before it reached Connor.

Sabrina (Brina) Killian—Nate's ex-girlfriend, who's a field agent with North Star and put together Connor and Nate's connection to the hit men North Star is tracking. Now with Connor.

Mallory Trevino—A North Star field agent sent to help Elsie and Nate when trouble starts.

Chapter One

Elsie Rogers only wanted to get back to her computer. She'd spent the past two days in a bunker on a farm, on someone else's computer. She hadn't minded that so much, until she'd been drugged. That had *not* been fine with her.

She'd been released from the hospital, shuffled back to North Star headquarters by Mallory, one of North Star's field operatives, but when Shay had walked into Elsie's office with that bad-news look on her face, Elsie knew she wouldn't be finding the peace of hacking anytime soon.

She'd only been sitting at her computer for about thirty seconds. It hadn't even booted up yet.

"How are you feeling?" Shay asked. Elsie loved having Shay as a boss. When she'd first started in the tech sector of the secretive North Star group, things had been a lot different. Granger MacMillan had been in charge and North Star's sole mission was to bring down the Sons of the Badlands, a dangerous biker gang.

Elsie knew all about dangerous men. So she'd been more than happy to aid the group, via her expertise with computers, to finally end the Sons. She'd moved her way up to head of tech in no time at all. But working with Granger McMillan had always made her nervous. He'd always been big, gruff and *very* serious. Like most of the men at North Star. She'd grown up not trusting any of those characteristics.

Elsie'd had to get used to the size and serious nature of the men in North Star, and thought she'd done a pretty good job. She'd even made some breakthroughs in her fears and anxieties when it came to men.

But she still preferred Shay as her boss. Even if Shay was just as lethal as any of the men there. More so, maybe, because Shay was the rare entity in North Star who didn't have a specialty.

She was good at *everything*.

"I feel great," Elsie said brightly, looking wistfully at her computer screen.

"We've got the name of the second target."

Oh, good. An assignment. Two of North Star's lead field operatives had been tracking two hitmen. North Star hadn't known anything about the gunmen or whom they'd been sent to kill. They'd only been tracking two shipments of illegal ammunition for guns they knew the mysterious hitmen used. The hope had been that they'd track it in time to stop the assassins from taking out their unknown targets.

Holden Parker, lead agent number one, hadn't found either target, but he'd helped save a woman whose parents were spies and were, in fact, connected to the hitmen.

Elsie wasn't a field agent in any way, shape or form,

but there'd been a computer on-site and she'd been sent to the bunker to see what she could find in the computer. Unfortunately, that meant being caught in the crossfire. Being tied up in that bunker by one of the spies who'd lost his grip with sanity had been a little too close to the terror she'd felt as a child trying to avoid her father's fists.

Now there was a second target. Work to do. Elsie could forget her terror and get lost in computer work once again. "What's his name? I'll give you everything there is to know."

Shay smiled, but it was not a real smile. Or comforting. At all.

"We don't quite know what we're dealing with yet," Shay said, and the fact they were so in the dark with this mission clearly bothered her. "Sabrina has some inside information on the second target, but we still have to be very careful."

Sabrina Killian, one of the other North Star lead operatives, was in the Tetons, tracing the ammunition and hopefully the hitman. She'd found the first target and was protecting him, and apparently had now figured out who the second target was.

Go Sabrina.

"Great," Elsie said, feeling a ripple of excitement. She'd been a little afraid Shay would keep her off duty for a few days to recuperate. "I'm ready to jump right into work. I swear. I feel fine. One hundred percent. Give me the name."

"That's excellent to hear." Shay took a deep breath, which wasn't a good sign. And she did not give Elsie the name. Then, even worse, she moved from her standing position to pull a chair up next to Elsie herself.

"Els, I'm going to need you to handle this one."

"Of course. Just give me the name." She had her fingers poised on the keyboard, but Shay shook her head.

Shay studied her very carefully. Elsie wanted to look away, *run* away, because this felt like bad, bad news. But she didn't move. She only stared back at Shay. She had learned a thing or two in her years at North Star.

"No, Els. I mean, you're going into the field."

"I can't go into the field." Elsie laughed because it was *crazy*. "I'm…I'm tech support."

"You're more than that."

"Okay, maybe, but I'm not a field operative. I don't know anything about going into the field! I went to try to hack that computer for you guys and got myself drugged and unconscious."

"That wasn't your fault, or because of anything you did. Look, this first part of the assignment doesn't require skills with a gun or hand-to-hand combat. It requires stealth."

"When have I ever been good at that if I'm not at the keys to the computer?"

Shay's expression went from sympathy and almost *apology* to stoic and cool in the snap of a finger. "You're the only one who can do this," she said, her voice hard. "Nathan Averly, our second hitman's target, is located in Blue Valley, Montana. His hometown, though he's currently at the Revival Ranch in their injured military recuperation center. Do any of those names or places sound at all familiar?"

Elsie heard a strange buzzing in her ears. It had been a long time since she'd had that particular shock reaction to something. But then again, it had been a long time since someone had mentioned her hometown to her. Here in North Star, her past didn't exist. No one knew, or acted as though they knew, where anyone else came from. The only time she heard her hometown's name was when she took time off around Christmas to visit.

She swallowed and, for the first time in her tenure at North Star, she wished she'd never joined. Wished she could lie with any capability. "I can't…"

Shay leaned forward. "I need you to, Els. You're the only one I can send without tipping anyone off. Born and bred in Blue Valley, and your sister is married to one of these guys running Revival Ranch. Small town like that? I bet you even know Nathan."

Elsie felt weak. "I…know of him." She knew more about his brother, Garrett. Because Garrett was a police officer, and had been a sheriff's deputy for Valley County when she'd lived in Blue Valley. That meant he'd arrested her father a few times before Dad had died, before she'd escaped.

Her father. Blue Valley.

It wasn't as bad as all that these days. Her two oldest sisters had built lives in Blue Valley. Dad was dead. Mom had moved. Elsie visited for Christmas because she loved her sisters and her nieces and nephews.

But this was work. A work her family didn't know she did. "Shay, I'm a terrible liar. You know this about me."

"I know. And I know it's a lot, asking you to lie to your family, but I have faith in you. You know I wouldn't ask you if I had any other options. I don't want you in the middle of this, but you're the only one who can go into a small town in Montana on a moment's notice and not create any suspicion. *Anywhere.*"

"But Nate... He'll know."

"Yes, he knows someone from North Star is coming. No, he doesn't know it's you. We've had to be careful about our contact with Nate, since we don't know who's after him or why. We don't know what could be tapped or overheard. But you would know. And you'll be able to help him research his theories without anyone knowing that's what you're doing."

"Shay, I don't think I can do this. I'm not...like you or Sabrina."

Shay put her hand on Elsie's shoulder. "I need you to do your best."

Elsie knew she was sunk. She couldn't disappoint Shay. Couldn't disappoint North Star. She managed a weak smile. "I guess I'm headed home."

NATE AVERLY PUSHED the cowboy hat off his forehead and wiped his face with the back of his arm. Hot one for a summer day in Montana. Reminded him of the Middle East, which almost never happened this far north.

A year ago, that might have set him off, but these days he focused all his confusion, anger and frustration into something else. He had a mission of his own. Not rehabilitation.

Retribution.

Something had ended his Navy SEAL career more than the explosion that had left him out of commission. He'd made a mistake, he understood that now. Trusted the wrong civilian. Followed the wrong lead. But being dishonorably discharged after his injury because of those mistakes had never made sense. Especially since his SEAL brother, Connor Lindstrom, had also gotten the dishonorable release when he had never done anything but join Nate on some security checks and questionings.

So Nate had never let it go. He'd dug. He'd collected evidence, and had almost a clear picture of what had happened. He just hadn't been able to prove it to anyone. Because when you were labeled *paranoid*, people didn't spend a lot of time looking into your theories, no matter how much truth they might hold.

Something more was going on. He'd received a very strange email from his former girlfriend. It had been in code—Nate was pretty sure—and had held enough of a hint to let him know she was involved in something.

Then he'd gotten her call, which he was still trying to understand.

It had also been in code. Nate's best guess: Sabrina had been trying to tell him she had somehow hooked up with Connor and that they knew Nate had sent a package, but it had been destroyed.

Nate had backups of what he'd forwarded Connor—he wouldn't have sent all that proof without having backups. But it worried him that Connor seemed to be the target of whatever was going on. Likely *because* of that package. That meant, if something happened to Connor, it was all Nate's fault.

If the man who'd also talked to him on that call had been Connor. *If* that's what Brina had meant.

There were just too many question marks, which made Nate edgy. About as edgy as the cryptic message that had followed: someone would be joining Revival Ranch to help him with his "quest."

He didn't know how to trust Brina's messages, but he did what he always did. He kept it to himself. He watched. He waited. And he did his ranch chores.

When he'd been a kid, scraping by on his family's small ranch at the southern edge of Blue Valley, Montana, he'd promised himself he'd never spend his adult life breaking his back at a failing spread.

Well, here he was doing just that. Though, in fairness, this ranch wasn't failing and was all about helping military men find their usefulness and emotional and mental health after injury.

His recuperation at Revival Ranch had been just that. A recuperation. His injuries healed, he felt sound in body and mind. The only thing that kept him here was what his therapist termed his *obsession*.

Nate scowled a little at that. He wasn't obsessed. He was determined. He was…focused. He had one singular goal—bring down those who'd wrongfully ousted him from the military—and he wouldn't rest until he'd achieved it.

Hardly an obsession. It was *justice*. Though the more time he spent at Revival, the more ways he understood there was no way to make his therapist or his brother fully grasp what had happened to him. They thought he was exaggerating. Twisting events and memories to suit this obsession.

He wasn't too far away from convincing them all he wasn't fixated anymore. It wasn't true, but he was closing in on making everyone—therapist, friends, brother and parents—believe he was letting things go.

The very opposite of what he was actually doing.

He heard the sound of a car far down the lane and immediately went on alert. The strange message he'd received had said someone would arrive to help him. Could this be his contact person? Was it real help? A trap?

Nate knew better than to abandon his work. That would give away his suspicions and, if this *was* someone after him, he wouldn't give them a clear read on things.

The dusty sedan pulled up in front of the main house. Though one of the men who'd founded Revival lived there, the Maguire house was the headquarters for Revival Ranch.

A small brunette stepped out of the car. He thought he recognized her, and even if he hadn't, she looked enough like her sisters that he knew she was a Rogers girl. Not a girl any longer, but in a town like Blue Valley, once a person had a moniker, it stuck.

Since the two older sisters lived here in Blue Valley, and she didn't look quite young enough to be fresh out of college, he pegged her as one of the middle ones. Billie or Elsie. His money was on Elsie. She'd been closer in age to him than Billie. Maybe three years younger?

Kyle Olsen came over and let out a low whistle, resting his body weight on the shovel he'd been using to clean out the stables. "Well, well, well. What do we have here?" he said, watching Elsie pull a purse out of the back of her car.

"Better watch yourself," Nate warned.

"Why?"

"Aside from the fact you're married?" Nate nodded his head toward the yard where the woman stood, oozing nerves. "Pretty sure if Jack hears you drooling over his sister-in-law, he'll take you apart limb by limb."

Kyle swore good-naturedly. "How many sisters-in-law he got? I've never seen this one before."

"Five Rogers girls." Nate couldn't remember the last time he'd seen Elsie Rogers, but that was definitely her. The Rogers sisters all had dark hair, dark eyes and slender frames. The older girls had always had an edge to them. The younger girls…the hollow-eyed skittishness of children who'd grown up in abuse.

She didn't head for the porch that would lead her to Revival headquarters. He tended to keep track of everyone's comings and goings, and knew that her sister Rose was in there with her kids. Instead of heading for her sister, though, she headed for him.

She walked across the yard, right up to where he stood next to Kyle. Kyle preened. Nate frowned.

"Hello, Nate," she greeted.

"Uh, hi. Elsie."

She released a breath. He couldn't tell if it was relief or something else. "You remember me."

It wasn't a question or an indictment or anything he could sort through. So he shrugged. "Sure. Hard to forget the Rogers girls."

Something on her face changed, but she forced a smile. "Sure. Well, I just came over because…" She cleared her throat, looked around at the men who were watching them carefully. Not just Kyle but two other soldiers who'd returned on horses.

Elsie focused on Nate and smiled, something like panic fluttering at the edges of her lips. "We have a mutual friend out there in the big, wide world."

"Huh?"

"Sabrina Killian? You know her, right?"

Nate blinked. After the strange email he'd gotten from Brina, he didn't think this was a coincidence. Any of it. "Yeah, I…did."

"I work with her."

It wasn't possible. This could not be the person he'd been waiting for. The help he was counting on.

Maybe he *wasn't* of sound body and mind, because if little Elsie Rogers was his contact to some secretive group that was going to help him because Brina had stumbled into this mess…

Well, Nate figured they were both screwed.

Chapter Two

Elsie wished she hadn't come over to Nate, but she'd needed to make some kind of contact. Now he was looking at her less like she was "one of those Rogers girls" and more like she was some kind of nightmare.

Definitely not the help he'd expected.

"I've got to go say hi to my sister and tell her I'm staying for a while. See you around." She nodded to the man who hadn't spoken at all, then Nate, and then turned on a heel to hurry to the main house. Rose hadn't been at her house, so Elsie assumed she'd be here helping Becca with something.

Elsie's stomach turned in awful knots. She had to lie to her sister, and everyone Rose and Jack worked with at Revival. She wasn't excited about doing that, but she definitely wanted to get away from Nate as soon as possible. He was tall and broad, with dark, dark eyes and an edge to him she didn't remember about the Averlys.

Maybe it had been his time in the military. Maybe it was this whole…being the target of an assassin. Maybe it was something else. But she didn't like edgy men with angry eyes.

"Wait a second." It was Nate's voice and he jogged up next to her before she could crest the stairs of the main house. "You know Brina?" he demanded suspiciously.

Elsie nodded. Sabrina. Who wasn't afraid of anyone. Who routinely kicked butt. Elsie had to give herself a shake. She might not be a routine butt kicker, but she was a North Star operative, one way or another. Being at home, she tended to forget what she'd built herself into.

She didn't have the luxury this time around. She had to focus on her task—her *mission*. She couldn't be the skittish girl she'd been here growing up. She firmed her shoulders and looked right up at Nate. Authoritatively. If she were pretending to be at a desk with her computer to protect her, no one had to know except her. "Give me a couple hours and I'll be able to get you on a secure line to her and Connor."

"Connor… So, it was Connor on the phone this morning."

"Well, yeah. Sabrina's protecting him. I'm…" It was ludicrous to say she'd been sent here to protect Nate. It would sound even worse to say she was his tech support. "My expertise is electronics. I'll be able to put you in contact with both of them without any chance of being traced or followed. I figure you have information that will be useful to put this mystery together."

"It's hardly a mystery," he said, but it sounded like he was talking more to himself than her. "They know where I am. They have to know where I am. The only reason Connor would be a target is…" He frowned. "What do you know?"

"Elsie?"

Elsie jerked at her sister's voice and couldn't fight the rising tide of embarrassment that would stamp itself in red blotches across her face. She tried to find her smile as she turned to Rose standing in the doorway, a fair-haired baby on her hip. "Hey, sissy."

The sight of her baby nephew she'd only seen outside of a phone screen once had Elsie forgetting all about her embarrassment. She rushed forward, flinging her arms around them both, Nate Averly and his uncomfortable energy forgotten. She looked at her nephew's wary face. "Look at you, peanut."

"Look at you." Rose studied her, a vague frown on her face. "It's not like you to text you're coming to visit and show up within a few hours."

Elsie worked up to looking into her sister's shrewd gaze. "I know. I'll explain everything." Somehow. "It's good to see you."

Rose maintained the frown but slid her free arm around Elsie's shoulders and pulled her inside. If she saw Nate, she didn't acknowledge him at all as she closed the door behind them with her hip. "I'm glad you're here. I'm just worried."

"Don't be. I have this project to work on, and I needed some…quiet."

Rose jiggled Xander in her arms. "You won't get that here, honey. Or at Delia's. Two kids under three in each place means scream city more than half the time."

"I know. I know. But you know, Montana quiet and family distractions in the evening so I don't get obsessed." Elsie had worked through her excuse and explanation on the drive from the airport. She took a deep breath and forced a smile. It was close to the truth. She wasn't lying. "That's why I was hoping to maybe stay in the little cabin on Revival property. I know you usually let the soldiers' visiting families stay there but—"

"I'll have to double-check with Becca to see if we have any families coming to visit, but I think we're clear there. Though it seems wrong for you to come all this way and not stay with me or Delia."

"Well, if it makes you feel better, I can just use the cabin as an office and spend nights with you or Delia. You don't want my computer stuff cluttering up your houses anyway."

"True. Baby debris is enough on the clutter score." Rose's analytical frown was still in place. "Els, are you okay? You look pale. And nervous."

"Yeah, I'm good. Really." Aside from the whole drugged thing, but Elsie wasn't bringing *that* up. "It's a really big project. It's new for me. I want to get it right. So I'm going to be a little…tightly wound. But that's why I wanted to be here. At home. Somewhere I could pull myself out of it when I get too deep in the obsessive part."

Rose led her into the living room, none of the worry leaving her face. "You've never called Blue Valley home before. Not since you left."

Elsie inhaled. She supposed she hadn't, and in that she hadn't been playing a part or lying. "You and Delia changed it for me." Her sisters had built real, good lives in the ashes of their terrible childhood. Hard not to find her affinity for the place knowing and seeing that.

Rose smiled. "All right. Let's go talk to Becca about

the cabin. She's got the rest of the kids locked in the office with her. But first, I want you to tell me why you were talking to Nate Averly."

"Oh." Elsie felt the heat creep back into her cheeks. She cleared her throat uncomfortably. "You never told me Nate Averly was one of the Revival men."

"I didn't know you knew Nate."

"Sort of."

"Honey, I know you're a grown woman and it's *none* of my business, but don't let a little flirtation—"

"Oh, no. *No.* No, no." Elsie laughed, knowing she sounded just a shade too close to unhinged. "No flirtation. We just recognized each other." Though that would make things easier, wouldn't it? If they pretended to have some interest in each other, as an explanation of why they would have to speak.

The knots in her stomach tied tighter. Who would believe Nate had any interest in her? How would she get through pretending without blushing like she was at just the thought? "He's...too big."

Rose snorted out a laugh. "In my experience, big men are not the problem." She squeezed Elsie's shoulders. "Just the mean ones."

"No, I know. I just..." She shook her head. This wasn't about their father. It wasn't about *anything.* Except lies. "I don't know what to say. I've got a big job to do. That's my focus." At least that was true.

Rose placed Xander in a playpen and then turned to Elsie, taking her by the shoulders. Elsie tried to keep her expression placid as Rose studied her.

"Promise me you're okay."

Elsie looked her sister straight in the eye, because this wouldn't be a lie, either. "I promise I'm not just okay, I'm good." This mission was a challenge, but at the end of the day, all she had to do was to lend her computer expertise to Nate.

It was important work. Work that might save lives. Including Nate's.

North Star had given her a purpose. A strength and confidence she hadn't had before. Between the therapy she'd gone through and the work she'd found to be her passion, she wasn't the same little abused girl that she knew her sisters sometimes still thought of her as.

Now she had a chance to prove it.

NATE DIDN'T CONCENTRATE very well the rest of the afternoon. He'd scraped his hands repairing a crooked stable door, and then spilled half a bag of feed and spent too long cleaning it up.

He'd listened to the gossip at dinner in the mess hall and heard Vivian, their cook and Jack's sister, mention something to Jack about Elsie staying in the cabin Revival usually used for visiting families now that Vivian had a place of her own.

So, that's where he was headed. He'd slipped out of dinner, hopefully undetected. If anyone questioned him, he'd say he had an upset stomach. It was a pathetic excuse, but he'd use it if he had to.

He could have waited for Elsie to approach him again, could have waited till dark to sneak over, but he didn't have the patience for it. He'd waited hours now.

And if he counted the time since Brina had called him through the ranch line this morning…

She hadn't given him any *real* information. It had been all code. If that. Just enough for him to *guess* Brina was with Connor, and that the evidence Nate had sent Connor a few days ago had been destroyed.

He had no idea *why* Brina was involved. No idea what Connor knew or what danger he was in.

This woman—*Elsie Rogers*—had more information than he did, and Nate didn't know how to deal with that. He'd thought he was in charge, the center, all this time and now…

Well, he'd get his information and go from there. Maybe he didn't have a ton of patience, but he'd recovered from the broken bones and torn cartilage and burns involved in being in an explosion. He knew all about slow and steady progress.

He walked across the property to the little cabin. In the distance, the mountains of his youth stood like sentries. He'd gone off to the Navy, not because he hated Blue Valley, but because he'd felt there was so much more out there.

Well, he'd certainly found it. And it had followed him home.

Nate gave one quick glance behind him, just to make sure no one was watching, then moved around to the back, which allowed the cabin to hide him from prying eyes. If he stayed till dark, no one would have to see him sneak back to the bunkhouse and then he could make up any excuse as to where he'd been.

He knocked on the door and waited impatiently.

When Elsie appeared, she seemed…different than she had this afternoon. She stood straight, kept her gaze level, and didn't blush at all as she gestured for him to come inside. The nerves he'd sensed radiating from her had been replaced by a cool confidence that felt a bit like whiplash.

"Did anyone see you come over?" Elsie asked.

"No."

"Good. We'll have to work out something about the time we'll need to spend together, but for right now, we can get down to brass tacks."

She closed the door behind him and he stepped into a cozy if sparsely furnished room. He hadn't ever had cause to be inside the cabin. His family was local, so when they came to visit, they didn't need a place to stay.

There were computers and computer equipment seemingly everywhere. Desktops and laptops and monitors. There was even equipment on the lone couch. It was like walking into some kind of command center.

"First things first, we're going to call Sabrina."

"I can't just call her. I don't know who's listening." He tensed against the look he knew was coming. That considering, slightly arrested look people gave a guy who believed in things like aliens. Or was obsessed over a discharge from years ago.

But she simply nodded, as if she agreed. "That's what all this is," she said, spreading her arm out to encompass all the equipment. "I know what I'm doing with tech." She pulled out a phone. "This can't be traced. This can't be tapped. You'll call Sabrina, and you two can exchange the necessary information. From there, I'll get the information we need to move forward."

She was clearly in her element. Confident when she hadn't been before. An interesting change.

"How do I know I can trust you and Brina?"

She pressed her lips together, as if considering. Her dark hair was straight as a pin, but looked glossy. Her brown eyes were deep and rich. She was a shade too skinny, and a few shades too pale, like she'd just gotten over some kind of illness.

He would know about that.

"I'm not sure I can prove to you that we're trustworthy. But the basics of it are that Sabrina and I work for a secret group. From the beginning of this group, our job has been to…take down the bad guys. Sounds cliché and kind of silly, but I don't know how else to put it. We're a network of people with different specialties. Sabrina is a field operative. I'm a tech operative. Sabrina was tailing a hitman when she connected with Connor Lindstrom. As they worked together to avoid the hitman, they put together a few things. Namely that the gunman was after Connor, and the logical connection was that it had something to do with Connor's dishonorable discharge from the military. That meant it had to connect to you, as well."

That certainly matched his current situation. "Brina called me this morning. Through the ranch line. But she didn't say anything worthwhile except hinted that the package I'd sent Connor had been destroyed."

"Yes, it was. Before Connor got his hands on it. What was in the package?"

Nate considered. While he did, she pressed the phone into his hand. "Look, you don't have to tell me. Yet. Call Sabrina."

Elsie had the number programmed in and all Nate had to do was hit Call. What else was there to do?

"Killian," a sharp, husky voice answered.

"Brina." He'd met Sabrina Killian when they'd both been in the first phases of working to become SEALs. Somewhere between that first step and the last, he and Brina had gotten involved. She'd been a whirlwind of energy, always ready for a fight, and Nate had been in awe of the woman *determined* to be a Navy SEAL.

Instead, she'd been severely injured in the Land War- fare Training phase. Her SEAL dreams dashed, she'd broken up with him in a fiery explosion of her own, then disappeared.

Nate had gone off to war, pride hurt but heart not mortally wounded, and he supposed that had been that. Brina had become another footnote in his life. A fond footnote, but not one he thought much about these days.

"Hello, Nate. How's it going?"

He eyed Elsie as Brina's familiar voice boomed in his ear. She'd always *boomed* or *sashayed* or *raged*. Something about her not changing set him at some ease. "Fine enough. Your friend is here."

"Els? Yeah, she's a gem. Be nice to her. There's no one like her, and she's going to be able to get you what- ever information you need. That, I can guarantee."

She certainly had the equipment for it. "Okay."

"You should talk to Connor. You two understand this

better than I do. But everything you tell him, he's going to tell me. We're working on this together."

"Brina…" Nate didn't even know where to begin. "This is serious. Dangerous."

"Yeah. Got it. Here he is."

There was the sound of shuffling, Brina's muffled voice, and then a deep, careful voice Nate knew as well as his biological brother's. Because Connor had become something of a brother to him in the SEALs.

"Hello."

They'd been on missions together. Been friends. Brothers. Kicked out of the military together.

Connor himself had told Nate to let the mystery go all those years ago when Nate had still been recuperating physically. So, Nate had begun to cut Connor off, slowly but surely. Not because he was mad. He understood why people thought he was crazy. But because he just…couldn't let it go. So, he'd kept everyone who'd thought he was nuts at arm's length. At least, until he'd had enough proof. Real proof.

Nate didn't know how to lead with any of that. "Care to explain how you got mixed up with my ex?"

"Care to explain why my friend's in the hospital and my cabin's obliterated? Oh, and why I got shot at?"

Nate winced. "I know you told me to let it go…"

"I told you to build your life. That's different. Sort of."

"Yeah, well…" Nate eyed Elsie again. Her fingers were flying over a keyboard. "You sure this is secure?"

"Positive," she said without looking up.

Nate sighed. "Okay, Brina's friend here says I can be

assured I can tell you anything without anyone being able to trace, hear, or whatever. I guess I have to trust her. I wanted to keep you as out of it as much as possible, Con. I tried. But this is bigger than me. Bigger than us. It's huge. We're talking military corruption on a scale…"

Connor didn't have to say anything. Nate felt Elsie's considering gaze. Felt Connor's frustration through the phone line. "I know I sound crazy," Nate said, irritated with…well, everything. "I know it. It's why I can't go to anyone. But I also know what I've found. What I sent you was evidence Rear Admiral Daria was selling off weapons to the highest bidder. It's what my informant back in the Middle East was *this* close to telling me. It explains everything."

Connor didn't respond, so Nate felt the rare need to fill the silence.

"I know it sounds like I'm making it up, but I'm not. After they kicked me out, all trails led to him. So, I dug. And dug. I finally got what I needed to prove it. I sent what I had to you because I wanted it in a secure place. I didn't want to involve you, but you were there. You were discharged. You were already involved. So, I sent you the evidence I had—"

"It's destroyed."

"Yeah, Brina told me. More or less." Nate paused. Did he really trust these people? Maybe Connor had gotten mixed up with the wrong "group." Brina being involved was confusing. Everything about this was… weird. Yet he'd always trusted Connor. He couldn't stop now. If Connor was the one to bring him down, maybe it was his just desserts. "I might have some backup of most of what I sent you."

"Nate…"

"You don't believe me."

"I've been shot at and my cabin was blown up. I believe you." Another long pause, but Nate didn't know how to fill this one. "I just don't know what the hell we're going to do about it. They want me dead. They're really going to want you dead."

"It's not the first time people have wanted us dead." But it was the first time they were specific targets, not just a uniform. And Nate didn't know why Connor would be more of a target than him. There'd been no shootouts, no explosions or things being burned down here.

Granted, Connor was isolated. Nate lived on a ranch with a bunch of military men. Still, Nate had been the one digging for evidence. Not Connor.

Was Connor meant to be his warning? Nate didn't know. Maybe he should have kept the evidence. Maybe… Hell, he didn't know. "I'm sorry you got dragged into this."

"I'm not." There was something strange in the way Connor said that, but without Nate seeing his friend's face, he didn't know what. "Have you seen any sign of people after you?" Connor asked.

"No. The only thing I can think of is that they want the evidence taken care of first. Before I sent it off to you, I think…someone was maybe out there. Watching. It felt like paranoia more than actual threat, though."

"You'd think they'd have a bigger…" Connor trailed

off, then exhaled harshly. "I know what I have to do. You sit tight. Watch your back. And let this…team of Sabrina's help you. They want to help."

Nate didn't trust Connor's voice, but Brina's *team* being little Elsie Rogers was… "They sent me their computer geek," he muttered, hoping she didn't hear him say it.

"Right, the person who could get us a secure line so I actually know what's going on. How dare they?" Connor said dryly.

"All I'm saying is you got the badass almost–Navy SEAL."

"Yeah, it's a real shame your ex-girlfriend couldn't come save your butt. Would have been a real nice reconciliation story."

Nate actually laughed, the idea was so ludicrous. "Brina and I would never reconcile. Whatever we had was all…kid stuff. Doesn't matter now." Why were they even talking about—

"Yeah, well, I slept with her."

Nate blinked. "I…" His mind was utterly blank. "I do not know what to say to that."

"Just felt like clearing the air."

Then he knew exactly what to say. Because this wasn't about Connor sleeping with his ex-girlfriend. It was about "clearing the air," which meant whatever Connor had to do was a little too close to a suicide mission. "Oh, no. No. Don't you go play hero, Con. No need to clear the air. No getting stuff off your chest. Because you're going to come out of this in one piece and tell me to my face you fell for my ex."

"I plan to. Listen to the computer geek. I don't understand this group at all, but I know they're doing the right thing."

"You sure about that?"

"Yeah. Yeah, I am." Connor ended the call, but Nate held on to the phone as if he hadn't.

Just because Connor trusted these people didn't mean Nate had to.

He glanced at Elsie typing away at her computer.

He could pretend. He'd grown very adept at pretending.

Chapter Three

"Well, that was informative," Elsie said brightly. She didn't know why she was pulling out the *bright* voice or pasting a smile on her face. Discomfort mostly, she figured. She'd listened in on his conversation. Obviously, she'd been right there, so he'd known she was listening. It wasn't eavesdropping, per se.

But Elsie had found out way more than she'd planned to find out.

"Was it?" Nate replied, staring at the phone as if it were a bug he wasn't quite sure whether to squash or let free.

"Sabrina didn't mention your…romantic history."

Nate pulled a face. "We were kids. Do I keep this phone?"

"I just meant…" She had no idea what she just meant. "Yes, keep the phone. Sabrina or Connor may communicate with you on it. They might not. But you can use it to make whatever calls you need to without fear of being traced or overheard. At least, through the phone. This Daria character. What do you have on him?"

He didn't say anything at first. She understood his reticence. They might know of each other from growing up in the same small town, but how was he supposed to trust some random woman who'd appeared, sent to help him by a mysterious group?

It was a lot to accept. Especially when the package was her…computer geek.

But the sooner they got started, the quicker she could be done lying to her family. The sooner the danger would be *away* from her family. Speaking of…

"Sabrina and Connor are handling the hitman after him, but there are two hitmen that my group are tracking. We've lost track of the second, though we're working with someone who was in contact with him. I don't see how he's not on his way here. If you can give me everything you've got on Daria, I can see if I can connect him to a hitman and we'll go from there."

Nate looked around the room at all the equipment she'd unloaded. She wasn't sure if it was a distrust of computers or her stamped all over his face, but it was clear as day.

"It's a lot to take in," she said, not without empathy. "I'd give you more time but, you know… Hitman on the loose and all."

"How do you know all this? Not you personally, but your…group. How is Sabrina involved? I don't—"

"Sabrina is part of the team. Has been for years. Longer than me, actually. Our goal has always been to do good in the world, but without always expressly having to follow the red tape law enforcement agencies do. That means our group was approached by another to partner with them to fully get to the bottom of a mystery of sorts."

"What mystery?"

"Well, that in and of itself is a bit of a mystery. Most recently, our group was tasked with stopping two hitmen. We followed one, which led Sabrina to Connor. Connor and Sabrina put together that you'd be the second target. I assume this Daria wants to silence you because of what you know." Elsie frowned at her computer, where she'd been catching up on the findings she'd missed while she'd been in the hospital. "The main thing that doesn't make sense to me is how Connor has been more of a target than you when it seems you're the source."

Nate stood there. He'd stopped looking at the phone, but he hadn't really moved. He was unnaturally still.

"Nate?"

He took a deep breath and blew it out. "I sent Connor the physical evidence I had. A few days ago."

"That means someone knew you did that." Elsie drummed her fingers on the desk. "But why not interfere before that point?"

"I sent it because I'd started to get the feeling I was being…watched. Followed. So I was careful. I sent the package with a friend who was going into town, to give to my brother, with directions to send it for me. If there really was someone following me, they wouldn't have caught it right away."

His brother. It was such a strange thing to be thrust into the middle of this. North Star and Blue Valley colliding. Computers in front of her, the ghost of her father's abuse hanging in the air. She could tell by Nate's careful look that he knew as well as she did that Garrett had arrested her father.

And many times, hadn't.

But that wasn't the point of why she was here. "So, you snuck the evidence out. How would they know to track it to Connor, then?"

"I don't know."

Elsie typed that question into the document she had on her screen full of questions. She wouldn't be able to find the answers to all of them herself, but it was good to keep track of them. "Is it possible they think Connor has the evidence, so now they don't need to mess with you?"

"I guess."

"You'd still be able to tell people. You still *have* the information. It might not be concrete enough for a trial or arrest, but—"

"No one believes me," he muttered. So low and grumbly, she barely made out the words.

"I'm sorry?"

He clenched his hand into a fist and let it go. "In the beginning, I tried to tell people. I tried to report Daria to whatever military and law enforcement entity I could think of. Everyone thinks I'm suffering from some sort of PTSD paranoia."

It was Elsie's turn to blow out a breath. "Everyone?"

"More or less."

Elsie knew he wasn't paranoid. She had too much evidence to the contrary. Maybe it was wrong, but it gave her more confidence she was actually the right person for the job. With her computer expertise, she'd help Nate prove what no one had believed.

"So, they've discredited you. You're harmless. But the evidence isn't, so they go after Connor." Elsie frowned. "All to keep quiet that this one guy was illegally selling military weapons?"

"He was. I *know* he was," Nate said. There was a heat to his gaze and an edge to his voice that made it easy to see why people thought he was paranoid.

She felt a little guilty for seeing it, but that kind of zealotry wasn't often accompanied by the truth. She had the uneasy feeling that maybe… Maybe this had more twists than North Star was banking on.

But she wasn't a field operative. Her job was to obtain evidence. Track movements. She'd do her job, and ideally arm North Star with not just Nate's take on things, but the true facts of everything.

She wasn't totally sold they were one and the same.

"Great, even you don't believe me."

"It isn't—"

"I have evidence."

Elsie looked up from her computer, eyebrows raised. "Have or had?"

He looked at her, those dark eyes edgy, broad shoulders tense. Like a man holding on by a thread.

Elsie's pulse scrambled. A mix of the kind of fear she'd never fully eradicate from her psyche, and something else she didn't fully recognize or understand.

She swallowed and held his gaze, no matter how nervous he made her.

"If someone was following me, if someone knew about that evidence and it going on its way to Connor, then someone could…" He gestured around the house and to her, and she understood he was worried her and North Star's involvement made him a larger target than he already was.

"No one can connect me to my group. As long as you don't go around telling people we're working together, no matter what anyone who's watching you sees, they can't connect it to this."

"Who's to say they're not listening?" He winced a little, like he understood that sounded like a very paranoid question.

"This cabin is a safe place. No one can listen in here. I've set up every precaution. We wouldn't want to be caught talking about evidence outside of it, but here, we can talk. I promise you."

"If someone is watching, won't they wonder why I keep sneaking in here?"

She'd found no other way around this. She'd tried. As she'd set up all her equipment, she'd tried to come up with every plausible story. But there was only one she could think of. "Well, I think we're going to have to make up a story about that."

"A story?"

"I think you're going to have to pretend to have an interest in me, Nate." She felt the heat of embarrassment sweep up her neck. "Sure hope you're a good actor."

NATE FOUND THE words didn't make sense. Not in any order he rearranged them in his head. "You want me to pretend..." He blinked.

"All I want you to pretend is some reason you'd be

hanging around this cabin. If you've got a better idea than…"

She was blushing. He couldn't force himself to look away from her face, where cheeks turned a pretty color of pink. It helped the slightly sickly pallor.

"Jack would kill me." That was the only thing he could think of to say. He didn't know what to do with… *this*. He'd given up hope of people believing him. Given up on anyone helping him to prove what he *knew*. He'd been working on this alone, in secret, and now suddenly there was a group, and little Elsie Rogers, and fake…interest.

"Right. Well, I guess you have to decide which hand you'd rather die by." Then she *smiled* as if that made any sense.

Nate had been perfecting his acting skills for years now, but they were failing him. So he had to rely on military stoicism. Mouth shut instead of hanging open. Keeping his spine stiff and ramrod-straight instead of fidgeting about. He had to wrap himself in the stillness of a Navy SEAL.

It might be the only way to survive this.

"You probably need some time to think it over. That's okay," she said gently.

He sighed because the world didn't always afford a man time to think things over, to act. To make the right decisions. Would he be here if he'd had time to think back in that Middle Eastern town where trust hadn't been thick on the ground? Between anyone.

No matter how gentle a person might be, sometimes a man had to make a choice. Best as he could.

"We'll build up to it. Rush in too fast, too many people will wonder, question, speculate. They'll pay too much attention to it."

"I'm afraid we don't have that kind of time," Elsie said. "Not with a hitman on the way."

"We'll have to make it. When I need to talk to you, or need the safety of talking freely, I'll find a way to sneak here. Probably at night. During the day, we'll see what we can do to be in each other's way. Look… interested in each other."

Interested in Elsie Rogers. Not exactly crazy, but his world had narrowed to a point. The point of proving his discharge was a lie. Proving he wasn't paranoid and someone *was* watching him to make sure he didn't get to the bottom of things. He hadn't thought about a woman romantically in…years.

He thought about Brina. And Connor. His friend had slept with his ex-girlfriend. And, quite honestly, he didn't know how *that* worked. Connor was honorable and, while he was a good-natured guy, he didn't put up with an unreasonable amount of attitude.

Brina was *all* attitude. Or had been. Maybe she'd changed. Nate himself sure had.

"Nate," Elsie said with a gentleness that made him bristle. Reminded him of therapy. "You said you have evidence Daria stole weapons from the military and sold them for profit," she continued, as if he didn't remember what he'd said. As if she was just another person carefully humoring him. "More than the physical evidence you sent to Connor that was destroyed."

Nate looked around the cabin. He'd familiarized himself with hacking as best he could, but he already knew she had him beat there. To move forward with this, he'd have to trust her, and he wasn't there yet.

Trust, like fake relationships, had to be built. Tested. So he'd build a test. "We'll talk tomorrow."

She frowned at him as he strode for the back door once more. "Nate. This is… I don't think you understand. There might be a hitman after you. Like *now*."

He'd been living watching over his shoulder for a while now. Felt scrutinized. Hunted. Played with. "They've had two years to kill me, Elsie."

That didn't seem to comfort her any. She stood, looking away from her computers and directly at him as she crossed her arms over her chest and stepped in front of the door he'd planned to exit through. "You don't know why they haven't pulled the trigger, so to speak, which means it could be anytime. The years before don't matter. Your friend was shot at. Not a year ago but *this week*. And from everything *I've* been told, the only reason he isn't dead is because Sabrina has been protecting him. If you're withholding evidence, you're risking…" She held up her hands as if she didn't have words for the magnitude of the situation. "Too much, Nate."

He considered. Rejected. Then moved past her. She moved out of the way rather than stand up to him. Just as he'd figured.

"We'll talk tomorrow, Elsie," he said. Firmer this time. Then he walked right out the door. And didn't look back.

Chapter Four

Elsie didn't plan to wait for *tomorrow*. Nate might hold a lot of the cards, but *she* had the means to get information at her disposal. Now that she had a name, all Elsie needed to do was start digging.

Rear Admiral Ronald Daria was, on the surface, unassuming Navy personnel. Spotless if sparse military record. Nothing particularly interesting about the guy.

But Elsie knew how to dig deeper, and then deeper still. She used all the information Holden had uncovered about Ross Industries—a group supplying weapons to elite hitmen—to cross-check anything potentially interesting about Daria.

She glanced up at the clock a little bleary eyed. She'd thought it had been about fifteen minutes, but it had been two hours. Still, in those two hours, she'd figured out Daria had been instrumental in putting military-grade weapons into the hands of Ross Industries.

It would be interesting to see what kind of concrete evidence Nate had, because most of what Elsie had dug up was circumstantial. Obviously, Daria had been careful. Though Elsie could find hints and lines to tug, it would take her even more hours to really locate anything concrete on Daria.

She was prepared to do just that—even if she had to stay up all night. Let Nate keep everything to himself. She'd present him with an entire dossier of all the evidence it had probably taken him those two years to collect.

She'd need some sustenance, though. No doubt tomorrow Rose would foist nutritious groceries on her, and Elsie would feel honor-bound to eat them, but for now she could live the way she preferred.

Sour gummy bears and an ice-cold Coke. The doctor who'd released her had said to hydrate. Coke was hydrating enough, wasn't it?

Before she could make her way to her suitcase and the snacks she had packed, a knock sounded on the door. Her first thought was that Nate had come back. Maybe with his evidence.

When she opened the front door, it was her oldest sister. "Delia." The world behind her was dark, causing nerves to skitter up Elsie's spine. Someone could be out there. "You didn't come out here alone, did you?"

Delia raised an eyebrow. "Was I supposed to come with an armed escort?"

"No, of course not. It's just late and dark and…" And Elsie should have gone to see Delia right away. The Shaw ranch where Delia lived with her husband wasn't that far away. She should have been the one to make the effort, but she'd gotten set up, then Nate, now Daria.

"Els, it's Blue Valley. Nothing ever happens in Blue Valley."

"Don't say that," Elsie said. It felt like a jinx.

"I guess that's not altogether true, but I'm safe. Are you?"

"Of course."

Delia peered around Elsie. "This looks…heavy duty."

"It is. It is, but it's not dangerous." Elsie had always looked up to Delia and Rose. They'd been tough in the face of the terrible childhood they'd had to endure. Delia had tried to take care of them, gotten them out of Dad's clutches one by one. She'd sacrificed everything for Elsie.

Now Elsie was standing here lying to her.

Delia surveyed the computer equipment with some suspicion. "I don't even know how to use my laptop."

"Sis…" She couldn't tell Delia what was going on. She *couldn't*. But the words were there on the tip of her tongue, wanting to tumble out.

"You're working. You don't want me to bother you."

"It isn't that." Though she should take that excuse. Let Delia believe that was the problem. Not lying. Not secrets. Not danger.

"It *is* that. And it's fine. More than. I like seeing you in your element, even if it makes no sense to me. But I want you to come over to Shaw for dinner some night this week, no matter how busy you are."

"Absolutely." Elsie swallowed at her tightening throat. "I bet Sunny and Gideon have grown like weeds. I want to see them. All of you. I do. I just…"

"Have important work to do. You don't have to feel guilty about that. We like seeing you be successful computer lady."

"But you worry."

"I'll never get over worrying about any of you. That's

just the luck of the draw." Delia pulled her into a hug. "I'm proud of you, and I'm glad you're home. Even if you stay holed up in this cabin for a bit at first." Delia released her and pointed a finger. "At *first*."

Elsie managed a smile. "I promise."

"Okay. I'll leave you to it, then." She surveyed the equipment one more time and shook her head. "Beyond me. Just beyond me." She walked back to her truck and, even though Delia was sure nothing ever happened in Blue Valley, Elsie watched until Delia was safely inside it and driving away.

Nate had to take this more seriously. He lived in the middle of all her family. Of course, an elite hitman *shouldn't* take out the wrong target, but no one could be sure, could they? A cold-blooded killer might kill anyone.

Why hadn't she gotten an update from Betty or Sabrina? It had been hours now, and there hadn't been a peep from any North Star people. Sabrina and her team could still be tracking the men after her and Connor. Elsie knew they had a whole team and they were in the Tetons—meaning a lot of wilderness in which to hide.

But there should have been an update. She closed the front door against the early fall evening chill and found her phone. She dialed headquarters first. When no one answered, it was the first real sign something was *wrong*.

She went down the list of people least actively involved with Sabrina's mission. Shay, Betty, Mallory. No one answered. By the time she got to Holden's cell, she was shaking with worry.

"Parker," he barked.

"Holden."

"Els. Hey. Things are a circus, can you—?"

"I've called everyone and anyone. You're the only one who's answered. What's going on?"

Holden sighed, which was odd. Even if he'd been through a lot this month, he was usually his over-the-top charming self. Not a stress ball.

"Sabrina's been shot."

Elsie dropped into her chair, her knees simply giving out. "What?"

"It's…bad. We're all working on this. Someone will update you when there is one."

"But—"

He'd already ended the phone call.

Shot. Bad.

It couldn't be true. Sabrina was…

Elsie inhaled a shaky breath. She'd been here before. Reece had been shot a few months ago. Granted, as part of the team on that mission, she'd always known what was going on. She hadn't been sitting there in the dark.

She glanced at her computer. She didn't have to be in the dark. Some hacking into the hospital system might give her more answers than anyone else had.

But if Sabrina had been shot, it was probably by the hitman after Connor Lindstrom. And there were *two* of them. One had to be moving on Nate.

This wasn't hypothetical anymore.

NATE LAY IN his bunk, tossing a baseball up and catching it as it fell. One of the coping mechanisms his therapist, Monica, had offered him. Do something familiar with his hands would help keep his mind focused.

His mind wasn't falling for it. His mind was on Elsie

Rogers, and Brina, and Connor. His mind was on all the things he'd uncovered in his years since discharge. Things that, for *years*, people had dismissed.

There was a relief in the fact that he was right, or that some people thought he was kind of right. But there was also a strange feeling of…anxiety. Who would he be if someone actually believed him? How would he proceed if Sabrina and Elsie and Connor actually followed all his leads?

A heavy, incessant knock sounded on the bunkhouse door. Since Olsen was closest, he glanced out the window. "Averly, it's that chick from this afternoon."

Nate got up off his bed. "How do you have a wife, Olsen? *Chick?*"

Olsen shrugged as Nate nudged him out of the way so he could answer the door. He was going to have to give Elsie a lecture about the appropriate time to have their conversations. Coming to his bunk that he shared with three other guys? Not it. Ever.

He opened the door, immediately stepped outside and closed it behind him so Olsen and the other two guys couldn't eavesdrop.

"You have to take this more seriously," she said without preamble.

"Take *what* more seriously?"

"This. You. There is a hitman after you, and you dismissed me. I let you dismiss me, but there's a hitman after you, and my entire family is wandering around and—"

"Slow down."

"No. I won't. People are in danger. *You* are in danger."

"Like I said before, Elsie, I just don't know why they'd shoot at me after all this time."

"Well, they shot Sabrina." She spat the words at him.

Nate didn't hear anything at all over the heavy thud of his heartbeat for a good few seconds. "What?" he managed to croak.

"I don't know if she's okay." Elsie held up her phone, like that meant something. "I don't have any clue as to what's going on because, instead of being at headquarters, I'm here babysitting you, and you won't even take the threat against you seriously."

She was panicking. That meant he couldn't. "Whoa, whoa, whoa. Back up." He had to get his facts lined up. This had to make sense.

"Holden said it's bad."

Nate didn't know who Holden was, but clearly someone who would know. "This hitman after Connor shot Sabrina?"

Elsie stopped her pacing and blinked. "I… Well, I don't know for sure *who* shot her. She's shot. It's bad. That's all I know."

"That's not enough information to go on."

"I have enough information to go on! There is a hitman after you. Unless just about everyone I work with is wrong—and they're not—there is a second hitman out there, and you are the most reasonable option for second target. Why wouldn't you take that seriously?"

He didn't know why that ticked him off. He'd been trying to get people to take him seriously for years. It was enough to drive a man crazy, and he'd been on the edge for a while. Now she was marching up to him, accusing *him* of not taking things seriously.

When Sabrina was shot and Connor was…what? Did anyone in her group care about Connor? Did anyone in her group care about anything? How would he know? Why was she demanding a response out of him in the *hours* after they'd met. When he'd been living with this for *years*?

No, she didn't get to be mad at *him*. She didn't get to lecture *him*.

He marched farther out into the yard, to stand in the glow of the outdoor light. "How's this for serious?" He spread his arms wide. "Come on, hitman. Take your shot."

Elsie's face went mutinous. It was fascinating, really. Maybe it was the shadows of the darkness around them and the lone glow of the outdoor light. Maybe it was the sheer strangeness of seeing Elsie so *angry*.

She stalked right up to him...

And punched him in the stomach. A surprisingly decent punch. If she'd been anyone else, he might have seen it coming and dodged, but since it was little Elsie Rogers, he took the blow in complete and utter shock.

"You're an idiot. And I don't like you," she said, shaking out her hand and vibrating with rage. A rage that had her storming off into the darkened night.

Nate managed to suck in a shallow breath and then another. Well, Elsie could certainly gut punch a guy.

And he kind of hated to admit it, but he'd let his feelings get the better of him. His frustration and his confusion, when clearly the real serious issue was that Brina had been shot. And it was bad.

All because of this thing with Rear Admiral Daria. *His* thing.

Nate scrubbed his hands over his face. For years, he'd been living with this. Alone. No one to share with, and then suddenly, out of nowhere, people believed him. People were involved.

Brina had been shot.

That meant, whether he liked it or not—whether he knew what to do about it or not—he needed to let some people in.

He went back into the bunkhouse. Olsen was at his heels immediately. "How'd you move so fast?"

"I'm not moving. I've basically known Elsie my whole life." He brushed Olsen off and knelt next to his bed.

"Known how?"

"Mind your own business, Olsen," Nate muttered. "Why don't you call your wife?"

Olsen didn't back off, but Nate couldn't care less at this point. Brina was shot and Elsie was mad and… He couldn't play it safe. Wasn't this what he'd been waiting for? Someone to *believe* him? Here she was, not just believing him but wanting him—*him*—to take this more seriously.

Yeah, it was time to stop being bowled over by this flip. He finally had what he'd wanted. He had to act on that. He dug out the folder he kept hidden under his mattress and tucked the flash drive that fell from it into his pocket.

He ignored Olsen's looks, noting that no one else really seemed to care. And then he went back outside. To find Elsie.

To do the thing he'd been waiting for the chance to do for *years*.

It was time.

Chapter Five

Elsie was so *furious*. At the situation, and worse, at herself. She paced the inside of the cabin, having to twist and turn around her tech equipment.

She'd never hit anyone before. She'd promised herself she never would. Oh, she'd done no damage to abs-of-steel Nate Averly, but she'd been a little girl who'd been used as a punching bag. Whether the blows hurt or glanced, they were an expression of anger that wasn't right.

It wasn't *right*. Sabrina had been shot. She'd punched a near stranger and told him she didn't like him.

Why had Shay trusted sending her into the field? She wasn't built for this kind of thing. She was the girl in the corner, nose pressed to the computer screen for a *reason*.

She plopped onto the couch and let her head fall into her hands. She was getting worked up, and she had to find some control. She did one of the breathing exercises she'd learned from her therapist when she'd been having panic attacks.

It was strange. She'd been a mess, drowning at her old job for a tech company. Not because the work had been hard. It had been a breeze. But because the world had felt too big and too scary, and the rote computer work hadn't challenged her in the least.

When Granger Macmillan had approached her—because of some paper she'd written in college, of all things—she hadn't trusted him at all. He'd given her a challenge: hack into a security-laden server.

She'd done it in ten minutes. He'd given her more tests after that, each one more complicated than the last. Even though she hadn't trusted him, the tests had become her center. When she lost herself in a *complicated* computer problem, she felt in control, confident.

Right.

When he'd finally convinced her to join North Star, she'd found a life she'd never had. She didn't panic in North Star. She rarely had nightmares. The work had given her something to hold on to.

She couldn't let that spiral out of control. She wouldn't let Nate or anyone else take that away from her.

If Nate wouldn't take this seriously, there were things she could do. Revival had its own security systems, but she could stealthily make them more secure. It was a big ranch, and there were too many places to hide, but she could make it harder.

She would. Not for Nate, but for her *family* and all the innocent people milling around this potential powder keg.

She was halfway through a remote diagnostic test on the security feed when someone knocked on her back door. It was late, so Elsie doubted it was one of her sisters again.

She went to the door. She couldn't see anything, but she doubted very much a bad guy was going to *knock*. So she opened the door. Nate stood there in the shadows. He stepped inside without a word. There was a folder under his arm.

"What's that?" she asked by way of greeting.

"My evidence against Daria."

He set the folder on the first free space he could find. "This is what I have."

She blinked. She'd gotten through to him. With a punch? She shook her head. No, punching him had not been right. "Before we…go into that, there's something I have to say."

His eyebrows rose, but he didn't say anything else. He just stood in the cabin, looking too big and far too edgy for any comfort.

Elsie wasn't *afraid* of him. Heck, she'd punched him and he'd taken it and hadn't even demanded an apology. Though he deserved one. "I'm sorry. I shouldn't have hit you. That was wrong."

"Are you worried you injured me?" he asked somewhat incredulously.

"Not in the least. It probably didn't even hurt, but expressing anger through violence isn't right. Ever."

"I'm going to have to disagree with you," he said somewhat flippantly. Then he winced and looked at her uncertainly.

Because the ghost of who she'd been was always front and center in Blue Valley—even if her sisters had reclaimed something here. She hadn't. "If we need to acknowledge it, we can."

He shoved his hands into his pockets and rocked back onto his heels, looking deeply uncomfortable. "Acknowledge what?"

She wasn't worried about his discomfort, she was worried about moving on so they could accomplish something. "My dad used to beat me and my sisters up. The town was aware. Your brother arrested him a time or two, but sometimes his hands were tied and he couldn't. I don't hold anything against anyone except my parents. My dad was the one who did it. My mom was the one who facilitated it."

"And someone should have done something. That's just the bottom line."

She wasn't sure it was better to hear that, or worse. Because no one had. She'd had to work through that, accept that no one had. "Sometimes there isn't anyone with the means to do something. That's just…the bad luck of the draw."

"Garrett…"

"Your brother tried. But the law doesn't make it easy to do much of anything without evidence or an adult willing to talk. I don't blame Garrett or, through extension, you, if that's what you're worried about."

"I wasn't…" He trailed off, frowning, but still with that aura of discomfort.

"That's the beginning and end of it. I'm just fine. Can we move on now? I'm not an abused little girl anymore. I'm an adult woman with a tough job, and I do some good in the world."

He studied her then nodded. "Then let's do some good. Together."

It felt like relief, but before she could enjoy even that small step forward, her phone rang. "Hello?"

"Hey, Els. It's Betty."

"What's the news?"

"It looks like Sabrina is going to pull through. It's a bad one, and she had to have some major surgery, but she's strong and stubborn."

"What about the others?"

"Still in the field. I'm at the hospital with Sabrina, so someone else will have to update you on that."

"I guess they will when they can." But it worried Elsie that everything was taking so long and she was so far out of the loop.

"Your assignment going okay?" Betty asked, but she sounded beat. Just exhausted.

"Go get some rest, Bet. I'll take care of my assignment just fine."

"Call if you need anything."

"Sure." But she wouldn't. She had to handle things on her own, and she would. For Sabrina in a hospital bed. For the little girl she'd been who'd thought she'd never have a chance to do anything. For her family— her sisters and North Star.

She said goodbye to Betty and hung up. She turned to Nate. "Sabrina is going to be okay. I guess there's still a small chance she won't be, but she's strong. She's… Sabrina."

"She's come back from bad odds before."

Elsie nodded. It helped to hear him reiterate her own

hopes. Sabrina would be okay. But that didn't mean the work was done. "Someone is coming for you, Nate. They have to be."

He nodded, his expression grim. "Let's see what we can do to stop them."

NATE COULDN'T EVER remember feeling true panic before he'd been discharged. Even when the building he'd been in had exploded, he hadn't felt *panic*. He'd been trained for that. He'd accepted the odds were he might not make it out of the SEALs alive. He knew what to do when all seemed lost.

What he hadn't been prepared for was the dishonorable discharge. People dismissing all his evidence. Friends and family, and even a licensed therapist, thinking he was unhinged. He'd accepted all that at this point. Even gotten used to it.

So used to it that trusting someone with everything he had… It felt insurmountable. So he kept the flash drive in his pocket and handed Elsie the folder. Even that had his heart racing as though he'd run a sprint out of a burning building.

She didn't say much. She looked through the papers, studying them with the weight they deserved. That was more than he could say about anyone else he'd ever showed them to.

"You hacked into his bank records?" she asked, eyebrows rising.

"Well, I paid someone to when I couldn't manage. I doubt that's all his bank records, either, but it's got some weird payments that coincide with some military operations."

She flipped to another page—presumably the one he'd cross-referenced with Daria's missions and where he'd been stationed. It was clear to Nate. Perhaps not the kind of evidence that could go to trial, but enough to prove Daria was shady.

Elsie was carefully analyzing the information, and he didn't know what to *do*. He felt like jumping out of his skin. Instead, he stayed exactly where he was, close enough to the back door he felt he could make a quick exit. Falling back on his military training and standing with legs apart, hands behind his back.

Like he was waiting for his dressing down.

"This is what you sent Connor?" she asked, flipping to the front and going through the papers again.

"Yes."

"It just doesn't seem like enough to shoot down a helicopter over," she said with a frown. "This is all circumstantial. You'll need something stronger to really pin it to Daria."

Nate thought of the flash drive in his pocket. He hadn't been able to bring himself to give it to her. There were just some things… He didn't have to trust her completely. What if she ignored it? Disproved it?

He could give her the info about Daria and work on the rest alone. Where it was safe. Where no one could tell him he was *reaching*.

"Yeah, but it's a starting point."

"Oh, it's more than that. But why go after Connor and not you? It doesn't make sense."

Nate didn't know what to say. He couldn't seem to come up with a lie that had become second nature to him when talking to his brother, his therapist, any of the guys.

With Elsie, the only thing he could think to tell her was the truth. Luckily that was terrifying enough, he just kept his mouth shut as she studied the papers again.

Her phone rang and he jumped at the sudden jangle, wincing at the weakness he showed by being startled by a *phone*.

If Elsie noticed, she didn't acknowledge it. She pulled her cell out of her pocket. "Rogers." She pulled up something on her computer, the phone tucked between her ear and shoulder as she typed away. Her dark hair had fallen out of its band. As whoever began talking, she sat a little straighter. Nate had to wonder if she was talking to some kind of superior.

She *was* pretty. He wasn't sure the last time he'd paid attention to the way a woman looked. The way he reacted to those looks.

So, you're going to do it now? That's healthy.

"What are my next steps?" she asked, pushing away from the computer. "All right…Sure…Take your time. Thanks, Shay." She ended the phone call then stared at him.

She swallowed and opened her mouth, but it took her a few seconds to actually form words. "They arrested Daria."

It felt a bit like a blow. Nate didn't know why. "What?"

"His whole team is wiped out." Elsie looked at her phone as if she didn't understand it. "Sabrina was the only injury. Daria is in custody, as is anyone who worked with him." She looked up at him. "I'll make sure the evidence against Daria sticks, so I guess…it's over."

Nate's stomach sank. He could let that be it. He could go back to the way things were.

But he knew things weren't over. He knew this didn't end with Daria.

He didn't have to tell her. He didn't have to risk it. But he thought of the way she'd come to his cabin, all worked up that he wasn't taking this seriously enough. That he was in danger. That her family could be caught in the crossfire.

If someone figured out he still had information—and that he might actually get someone to believe him about it—he'd be in danger, yes. But so would the people around him.

Maybe even Elsie herself.

If he couldn't trust *her* with it—or the group who'd taken down Daria when no one else had or would—then there was no hope. He might as well give up.

He closed his eyes and sighed. "No, Elsie. It isn't over." There was no turning back now. If Daria was taken down, great, but to do the rest, he had to accept he was going to need help. And it looked like Elsie was his help. "Daria was just the beginning."

Chapter Six

Elsie didn't know if she had any surprise left in her. Between being home in a North Star capacity, Sabrina of all people being seriously shot, and this Daria already being taken down with no help from her, she was already reeling.

Now Nate was standing there grimly saying...

Elsie shook her head as if that might clarify things. "I don't understand."

"When I was looking into Daria, I found more. Bigger. He was a small cog in a big, messy machine."

"You mentioned military corruption on the phone with Connor. But I thought..."

"That I was crazy?"

She glowered at him. "Why is that the conclusion you keep jumping to? Why can't you give me five seconds to work through anything without assuming everyone thinks..." It dawned on her then.

Everyone *had* thought he was paranoid. No one had given him any credit. No matter what he'd found, he'd spent a while being dismissed and discredited. That kind of thing... Well, she knew what it was like. But even when she'd been living through it, she'd had her sisters. They'd built their own little world of belief.

Nate was alone.

Elsie was not tough like the North Star field operatives. She had too soft a heart for a sob story—and Nate sure had one. She knew he wouldn't appreciate her feeling sorry for him, but it didn't eradicate the feeling.

"No one has believed me in a very long time," he said, his expression intense but also…defeated. Like he'd given up. "Not my family. Not anyone here. Why would you believe me? Why would *anyone*?"

"I guess sometimes the people who know you, who care about you, have to worry. Naturally. Honestly. And it…colors their perception of…well, what's going on."

"A lot of things have colored their perceptions," he said, an edge of bitterness to his tone.

"But I don't have any of that. I just have the facts, and the facts I have back you up." He looked at her, those dark eyes just a little wide, as if surprised, even standing here surrounded by her computer equipment. But they didn't have time for his reticence or surprise, and she had to remember that. "So if you've got more information, you need to give it to me. You need to stop holding back. I can't help you if you're keeping little pieces of things hidden because you're afraid I won't believe you."

He straightened, his frown turning into a deep scowl. "I'm hardly *afraid*."

"What would you call it?" she retorted, looking at him expectantly.

"I…"

Elsie waited. Maybe she should have said something out of kindness. Changed the subject so he didn't have to flounder. She'd been afraid too many times to count. She knew how that could warp your perception of the world.

But she needed him to understand what he was doing—and why—so he'd stop. So North Star could do what it set out to do—stop the bad guys. If Daria wasn't the only bad guy out there…

She huffed out a breath. They didn't have time for *any* of this. "We have a lot of work to do, Nate. It doesn't matter if it's fear holding you back, or some amazing courage I couldn't even begin to fathom." Though she knew it was fear. "You have to work with me. Or there's no point in me being here. Sabrina was shot for nothing. Maybe I could figure this out without your help—but it would take time. Time we don't have. There's still a hitman on the loose."

"If they really wanted me dead, they could have done it already."

"Do you want to wait around to figure out if they will? Maybe you'd like me to figure out why they waited—you know, after they kill you."

He shook his head, but she could read some conflict inside him. Even as he told her no, he was letting her words sink in. He was weighing the importance.

"I need time," he said, his voice a rough scrape.

Elsie didn't groan in frustration. Sometimes you had to beat your head against a brick wall a few times to make it through. Hacking and her computer work was often painstaking. Running into blocks over and over again and trying new things until there was a break-through. She could beat his stubbornness.

She had to. "You don't have time. Beginning and end of story."

He jammed his hands in his pockets, scowling. "Well, I never thought I'd be bossed around by little Elsie Rogers."

"And I never imagined I'd escape Blue Valley and be someone who *could* boss people around." She took a moment to fully absorb her own words. No, she never thought she'd be here. But here she was. She wouldn't be afraid of it. "Sometimes change is a good thing."

"I hope you're ready to prove it," he muttered. He pulled one of his hands from his pocket and held out a flash drive. "This is two years' worth of work. Everything I have. I only sent Connor the things on Daria, but whoever is above Daria wouldn't necessarily know what—*if* they know I have anything. They'd only know I sent stuff, and if they knew what I had…" Nate shrugged.

She took the flash drive, relief that he'd hand it over and satisfaction she'd gotten through to him coursing through her. But his words made it clear. "The timing means they know you know. You sending that package to Connor was the tip-off."

She could tell he didn't like that, but with all the information at her disposal, it was the only sensible conclusion.

"Fine. They know. They acted because I sent information. We'll work from that hypothesis…for now. They wouldn't know I didn't send Connor everything."

"Why didn't you?"

"I didn't think he'd believe me if it was too big. A lot of the stuff I have pointing to a bigger organization is circumstantial. I just needed one person to believe me, to work with me. Connor was already involved, so it had to be him. I was going to take it step-by-step. Daria first."

Elsie couldn't blame him there. "You sure this is everything?" she asked, holding up the flash drive. She didn't know if she'd believe him even if he said yes, yet she had to ask.

Nate nodded. And he looked mad enough that she was compelled to take that as the truth.

So she put the drive in the computer and got to work.

"NOT BAD FOR an amateur," Elsie said, her nose practically pressed to the screen. She'd spent silent minutes pulling up everything he'd saved to that drive over two years. He'd had to pace the room to keep himself from demanding what she thought.

"Gee, thanks," he muttered irritably. When was the last time he'd been an amateur at something? But that's exactly what he felt like while she sat there fingers flying over the keys of her computer like some kind of fairy princess of tech.

She blinked up at him, almost as if she'd forgotten he was there. She scratched a hand through her hair then stretched, the material of her shirt stretching over her—

Nate looked down at the floor. Yeah, being attracted to her didn't work on *any* level. There was clearly something wrong with him, but he didn't have to succumb to it. He would stare at the floor and escape as soon as he could.

"Since you don't know how to do it stealthily, the biggest problem is that anyone can see what you're doing and immediately delete or change the information you're collecting," she said. "Every time you saved something, they probably knew. Now, they might not have always known it was you, but they didn't need to. They only needed to alter the information so whatever you saved no longer looked real."

The words had him forgetting about her stretching. His gaze jerked up. "Is that why no one believed me?" He'd sent proof—or so he'd thought—to everyone he could think of in the Navy, and gotten nothing in response. Except a call to his therapist here.

If the information had already been changed, that made him look as unstable as people seemed to think. And there was a *reason*. Not just people's distrust in his stability.

Elsie shrugged, nose pressed to the screen again. "Probably. I mean, if someone thought you were even kind of right, they could start digging and see what's been changed, but someone would have to want to do that. My guess is, going against the brass—especially someone like Daria who has nothing bad in his record— isn't something most people are willing to attempt without solid, irrefutable evidence. Unfortunately, someone probably made your evidence look really refutable."

"So…" It worked through him then. That it might not just be as simple as his friends not trusting him enough.

That it might actually be people working against him to discredit whatever he found.

Could it be true? It all seemed far too good to be true.

Except that Sabrina had been shot—no matter that she might survive. Brina had been through enough. She shouldn't be caught in the crosshairs of this...

But if she had been, didn't that lend credit to everything he believed? Finally?

Elsie leaned away from the screen, blinked her eyes a few times and sighed. "This gives me a place to start. I might be able to uncover what they changed, when, how, who. That will be the next step. Who's above Daria?" She yawned as she asked the question.

"It's the middle of the night. Don't you sleep?"

She waved that away. "Don't need much usually. Doctor said I might be more tired than usual, but I can push through. Plenty of supplies." She pointed to the two empty pop cans next to her.

Nate couldn't think about the fact her "supplies" apparently meant sugar. "What do you mean the doctor said?"

"Oh. Right." She shifted in her chair uncomfortably. Her attempts at being casual failed miserably, and she kept her eyes on the screen though he didn't think she was actually looking at anything. "Just a little...incident a few days ago."

He folded his arms across his chest. "Why don't you explain that?"

"It doesn't matter."

"Explain it," he insisted.

She rolled her eyes and huffed, glaring at him. "It's

nothing. I wasn't shot, like Sabrina. I don't do field work. Mostly. I happened to be on-site trying to hack a computer and...someone drugged me."

"You were *drugged*." It explained the sickly pallor, but what the hell was she doing working this hard when she'd been drugged. And apparently not that long ago?

"It's really not that big of a deal. I don't even remember it. I feel bad for Willa. She's the one who had to witness her dad losing it. Willa, she's... It's complicated, but basically her dad was a spy who lost it a little and was ready to...well, kill us all, I guess. So, she had it way worse than me. Her own father was going to kill her."

Nate couldn't help but stare at Elsie. Hadn't her own father been capable of the same? And why did their conversations keep coming to this awkward place where he knew...exactly what she'd been through?

She said she didn't blame anyone, but Nate didn't understand how that could be possible. How she could still think someone else had it worse than her.

Something on her face softened and Nate didn't know why that was so hard to look away from.

"You know, your mom tried to help us once."

"What?"

"She brought a meal over. It was after Garrett had arrested my father, one of the times he did that didn't stick. You know that old sheriff—my father was buddies with him or whatever. He'd find a way to wiggle Dad out of things, and CPS could never find any evidence. But Garrett arrested Dad anyway this time. It must have been his first year with Valley County. I was pretty young. Anyway."

"Garrett is sheriff of Blue Valley now. He actually… got community support to start a Blue Valley PD instead of be patrolled by the county."

"Is he?" Elsie actually smiled. "I'm glad. He'd be a good one. Hard to believe he'd have a whole department."

"Oh, it's only him and Mrs. Linley as dispatcher." But that wasn't what he really wanted to talk about. "My mother…?"

"Oh, right. Garrett must have told your mother about it. She came over, brought us dinner. A chicken noodle casserole. It smelled amazing."

Nate's stomach felt like lead. Since he'd never known his mother had done such a thing, he had a feeling this didn't have a happy ending.

"You must have been in the Navy by then, and Rose and Delia were gone. It was just the three youngest of us, I think. Your mom told my mother she could take us to Billings right then and there before Dad came back." Elsie smiled, even though, clearly, her mother had not gone. "My mother refused, of course. Threw the casserole in the trash. But your mom tried."

Nate didn't know what to say. It sounded like his mother. She was not a particularly effusive, friendly woman, but she believed in right and wrong.

"My mother never left, even when people offered help. She always told Dad, and then Dad wouldn't drink or knock us around for a few weeks while he waited for someone from CPS to show up—usually if someone

came by trying to help, CPS would come out as soon
as they could. But my father knew how to work around
the system. And when you're as isolated as Blue Valley,
he always had warning."

"I don't know what to…say."

"You don't have to say anything. It's not…poison.
You know? I'm not going to fall apart if you mention it.
If *I* mention it. There were people like your mom who
tried to help. Like Garrett. There's just only so much
you can do for five girls whose parents don't want the
help that's being offered."

"There should be more."

"There should be. And sometimes there is. I've
helped kids. Kids stuck in worse situations than even
I was in. He didn't win, and you don't have to act like
I'm more fragile because of it. That's why I tried to
clear the air earlier."

"I don't think you're fragile."

"Good."

"But if you were *drugged* not that long ago, maybe
you should rest."

"Maybe I should, but Sabrina was shot today. Betty
said she's probably going to make it, but there's still that
probably. There's a hitman somewhere, and you're the
likely target. You live among my family and friends.
I'll rest when we figure out how to make sure everyone's safe. How can I rest before that?"

"I was a Navy SEAL. Even we rested sometimes."

"Well, feel free to go rest, Nate."

He scowled. He was hardly going to *go rest* and

leave her to do all the work on her own. "What can I do?" he demanded.

Elsie studied him, a frank appraisal that made him want to fidget. Since he *had* been a Navy SEAL, he didn't. But it was uncomfortable, that impulse.

"Notes," she said with a nod.

"Notes?"

"Yes. We're going back to high school, Nate, because I'm going to need you to write down and organize everything I tell you. Do you think we can get a whiteboard?"

"A whiteboard."

She waved it away. "We don't have time. Paper will do."

"I was not a good student."

She flashed a smile at him, one that had some uncomfortable tightening passing through his body. "I'm sure you'll figure it out. I've got faith in you."

No one had for a very long time, and Nate found he didn't know what to do with it. Except do as she said and take...notes.

Chapter Seven

Elsie woke with a pain in her neck, and what felt like a keyboard pressed to her face. As she straightened, she realized that, yes, she'd used her keyboard as something of a pillow.

Not the first time.

She rubbed her face as she yawned and looked around the room. She startled when she noticed Nate on the corner of the couch he'd cleared off so he could sit to take notes. The notebook was in his lap, the pen was in his hand, but he was fast asleep.

His head was tilted just slightly, his eyes were closed and his breathing was slow and even. She got the feeling that if she moved, he'd jump to alertness in the snap of a finger, so she found herself sitting very still.

His dark hair was messy, and a day's growth of stubble gave him an even more dangerous look than he usually had about him. She would never have considered him *her type*, what with the sheer height and breadth of him, but he was objectively handsome.

The flutter of attraction in her chest was so novel, she just stared at him. She'd had boyfriends before…in college. She'd made a point of it. But working at North Star the past three years, and all the problems she'd been having at her previous job before that had taken up all her time, and male companionship had fallen to the wayside.

And why on earth are you thinking about male companionship on a job, with a man from your hometown?

As if he'd read her thoughts or sensed her staring, Nate's eyes blinked open. Elsie knew she should look away. Her mind screamed at her to, but she just couldn't seem to take her gaze from his sleepy dark one.

"Fell asleep, huh?" he said, his voice rumbly.

Her stomach did a strange swooping roll, like she was on a roller coaster. Before she could say anything, a knock sounded at the door. Elsie jumped a foot. Oh, this was not good. "You have to—"

"Disappear," he finished for her. He was already up and heading for the back door.

Elsie swallowed at the nerves battering her. So many different kinds of nerves, she didn't even know what to do about them.

The knock sounded again and Elsie went to answer it. Nate was slipping out the back, but Elsie needed to create a little bit more time. She opened the door a crack.

Elsie's eyes widened. "Rose," she squeaked. "It's early."

"Yeah." Rose studied her skeptically through the crack. "Open the door, Elsie."

Elsie made a big production out of it, going as slowly as she could and hoping any evidence of Nate was long gone.

Rose stepped inside, frowning.

Gabrielle wiggled and held her arms out to Elsie. Elsie took the toddler and smiled winsomely at her older sister.

"What are you hiding?" Rose demanded.

"Nothing. Nothing!" Elsie jiggled Gabs in an attempt to get her niece to laugh.

Rose was clearly not convinced. She walked deeper into the cabin, little Xander peacefully asleep in his chest carrier.

"Doughnuts!" Gabriella shouted, boisterously wiggling in Elsie's arms.

"Yes, we brought doughnuts," Rose agreed. "But this is not a place for children. You could have said that instead of acting all weird about letting us in."

Elsie looked around at all the equipment. "Sorry, I fell asleep at my computer last night and I'm just...out of sorts. Sorry."

Rose reached out and touched her cheek, and there was that *worry* Elsie had needed to stay away from. She loved Rose and Delia with all her heart, but the real reason she avoided Blue Valley these days wasn't the ghost of her father, it was *this*. Being treated like she couldn't handle anything.

"Don't be sorry. What's really going on with you, Els?"

Elsie swallowed. "I told you. This project..."

"If it's making you this jumpy, and has you falling asleep at your computer, maybe..."

"Don't do that." Elsie stepped away from Rose's hand, trying to keep her voice even since she was holding Gabrielle. "Don't underestimate me."

"I'm not," Rose said, sounding hurt.

"I can handle my life. Sometimes it means falling asleep while I work. Sometimes it means…" Well, it was no time to bring up Nate. "I'm capable. And an adult."

"I know."

"Do you?"

"Yes," Rose said, still sounding hurt. "You could do anything, Elsie. I believe that for all of us. If I can be *here*, married to Jack, mother of his children. Mother, period. I think any of us can do anything. But…I don't want you pushing yourself so much you end up… It isn't always healthy to work so hard."

"And sometimes it is. Sometimes you put in the hard work because the outcome is worth it." Elsie nuzzled Gabs. "I know kids and work aren't the same, but it's similar. I've watched you and Delia enough to know that being a mother—a real mother—is hard, hard work. But you do it."

"Yes. Because they're living, breathing human beings who don't give you much of a choice."

"We know there's a choice. We saw the other side of that choice."

Rose sighed. "I worry about you girls. I can't help that."

Elsie knew she couldn't, but she also thought if she could *show* Rose all she did, maybe Rose would get to that point.

Would Rose ever really believe she could handle Nate Averly, though? Elsie barely believed it herself. But she had a job to do. A *job*. "This job saved me,

Rose. I need you to understand that. As much as you and Delia did."

"I didn't—"

"As much as you and Delia did," Elsie repeated. "So, I need you to trust me when I say I know what I'm doing."

Rose nodded. "Okay. Okay. I'll back off." She glanced at the computers once more, then frowned, picking up the notebook on the couch. "This isn't your handwriting."

Elsie did everything she could—channeled every North Star field operative she'd ever worked with—to keep her face impassive while her mind scrambled. "No, it's notes on the project I'm working on from…my boss." She even managed a smile as she lied to her sister.

Rose shrugged and dropped the notebook.

Elsie knew she should beg Rose off so she could work this morning. She wasn't sure where she and Nate had left off. Apparently, they'd both conked out when it really hadn't been an option. She had to focus on Nate and the potential hitman after him.

But a girl had to eat. Especially doughnuts. "Is it warm enough to eat those doughnuts on the table outside?"

Rose smiled. "Yeah, we can do that."

NATE KNEW HE'D made a tactical mistake last night. If he hadn't fallen asleep, he might have been able to sneak into the bunkhouse before the first early morning alarms went off, but even that would have been difficult.

He did live with a bunch of former soldiers.

The real problem was that he shouldn't have stuck around Elsie's and taken notes. He really shouldn't have allowed himself the luxury of falling asleep on her couch—not that he felt like he'd *allowed* it. He wasn't sure how it had happened. One minute he remembered her talking about some group she'd worked a mission on—and she'd said *mission* with all the seriousness of a military general—and the next...

Waking up to her dark eyes staring right at him, and that pretty little blush creeping up her neck and—

Nope.

Nate pushed into the bunkhouse knowing that most of the guys would already be up and at the mess hall eating breakfast. Even if they didn't care, they would have noted his absence last night and this morning.

And they'd be forming their own conclusions— conclusions that would likely get him into trouble with *someone.* Whether it was his therapist, or Elsie's sister, or her brother-in-law.

Nate could have explained it away in any number of ways, *if* Olsen hadn't known Elsie had come to the door last night. And Olsen had a big fat mouth.

Nate ran through the shower and got dressed. He had no choice but to follow his usual routine for the day. Breakfast at the mess hall, his therapy session with Monica, then whatever ranch chores were on the docket.

When he got to the mess hall, he ignored the way it felt like all eyes were on him. He might not be de-lusional, but the paranoia thing wasn't always so easy to dismiss.

Nate made his way through the food line then took a seat at a table with only two other soldiers.

"You work fast," Drake Worthington said, looking up at Nate with a grin.

"Don't know what you mean."

"Yeah, you do," he said with his booming laugh. "And Olsen's told everyone—not just our bunk."

"Told everyone *what*?"

"That you spent the night in a cabin with Jack's sister-in-law."

Nate scowled. "Olsen's a liar."

"You weren't in *our* bunk."

"I didn't realize that made Olsen a great teller of truths."

Drake shrugged, and Nate knew he hadn't gotten anywhere in convincing him the truth was not the truth. But he didn't dig himself a deeper hole. He did what he did best. Kept his big mouth shut.

He ate his breakfast and headed for the stables, where he did most of his therapy with Monica. Equine therapy was the staple of Revival Ranch, and he knew it was a draw for a lot of the guys.

But since he *wasn't* paranoid or delusional, it didn't do a damn thing for him. He'd come here only because his family had all but begged him to.

"Morning," Monica greeted in her efficient, friendly way. For the whole of the time he'd been here, Nate had tried not to take his frustration out on Monica. Deep down, he knew she was doing her best, but it was hard not to lay all his emotional baggage at the feet of the person always so bound and determined to bring it up.

"Morning," he offered. Their usual job was to saddle up whatever horses would be needed for work that day, then take them out to the various stations while the men who did the morning ranch work and had their therapy sessions in the afternoon were waiting.

Those men would rub down the horses in the afternoon, or exercise the ones that didn't get used. Revival was a well-oiled machine, and between Monica doing the therapy work, and Becca Maguire acting as the organizer and stand-in when necessary, Nate had to step back and admit that what they'd built here was something pretty impressive.

But that didn't mean he enjoyed being a part of it.

"Nate. Where were you last night?"

Jerked into his current reality by that question, he tried to tamp down his annoyance. "What's it to you?"

She didn't answer his belligerent response, just cinched the saddle onto the horse. "You know, if you want to leave the ranch, there are protocols to follow. Letting someone know where you're going is top among them. For your own safety."

"And yet I'm fine," Nate returned.

He *knew* he tested Monica's patience, but she never showed it. Not in any way he could see. He should give her credit for that—a thought he hadn't had this whole time. But there was something about Elsie believing him that made him look at everything in a new, less uptight way.

In fact, he found himself coming up with excuses. They might be lies, but usually he'd just firmly refuse to talk to Monica. Or his lies were specific to getting her to believe he was doing better. But these lies were just a cover-up. To keep the focus off Elsie.

"I was going to take off. Go to Garrett's or my parents'. Somewhere… I just needed some quiet. To work through some stuff. I realized, belatedly, I went about it the wrong way. I just didn't think you'd approve me being alone, so I didn't seek out approval. I should have at least…discussed it. With someone."

Monica nodded and they worked together to secure the next saddle, giving each horse a little treat once they were finished. When Monica finally spoke, it was in a calm delivery that totally belied the words she spoke.

"What about Elsie Rogers?"

"What about her?"

"There's talk. And while I usually ignore gossip—especially of this variety—I was concerned."

Damn you, Olsen. "I don't know what you're talking about."

"There's talk you spent the night in Elsie's cabin."

"Talk from Olsen. We both know you can't trust that guy."

"It's not just Olsen, Nate. But it's the kind of gossip that can make everyone's life a little harder. Elsie isn't part of the ranch."

"I'm well aware. I've known Elsie my whole life. Probably know her better than you do." He had to keep his hands gentle for the horses, but it was a hard-won thing. If anything these therapy sessions had given him, it wasn't healing. It was the ability to control an emotion.

Isn't that part of healing?

"Which means what exactly?" Monica asked, bringing Nate out of his thoughts.

"It matters to you how?"

Monica sighed, and it wasn't frustration on her face. It wasn't any of the things he'd expect, just that infinite well of patience and something that had always made him edgy. Concern.

"I know you don't believe it, Nate, but I am on your side. I want to help."

For a year he'd been here, having these sessions with Monica, and he'd always viewed her as the enemy. But he realized…knowing someone out there was changing any evidence he found, having Elsie offer him some belief…Monica really was just doing her best with the information she had.

Someone was working against him. Maybe not specifically—maybe not with the intent to make everyone in his life think he was off-balance. But by covering their tracks, he constantly looked delusional. And thinking, on occasion, he was being watched didn't help matters.

Because he wasn't always sure he was.

But Connor was targeted after you sent stuff, even though you were sneaky about it.

He wasn't unhinged, and he'd spent a lot of time being angry at the people around him for thinking he was. If he actually took a breath and put himself in Monica's or Garrett's shoes… Why *should* they believe him?

Would he?

And he knew, with a clarity he didn't particularly appreciate, he would have done the same as Garrett and Connor and tried to offer help in a way that did not bring up all the wild stories Nate might *know* were true but couldn't prove.

Elsie could. He had to believe she could prove it.

Nate stopped what he was doing and summoned all his calm, all his renewed faith that everyone *wasn't* right about him. He actually did have a good enough head on his shoulders. He'd need to access that to convince Monica what he needed.

He could leave Revival without her permission, but his life would be way easier with it. "I want to take a break. From Revival. I think it'd be good for me. And, you know, maybe when I get back, Elsie will be gone again and these dumb rumors can die off."

Monica studied him, and he knew she was carefully considering his words. He might not *like* therapy, he might have often taken that dislike out on Monica, but he knew she was a good person. A good therapist. If he dug under all his own issues, he believed she wanted to do the right thing.

She shook her head. "I don't think it's in your best interest to go somewhere alone."

"Fine. I'll drag…Garrett along." It would require lying to his brother, but a plan was beginning to form. One no one in his life would like. Including Elsie.

So, he just wouldn't tell her.

Chapter Eight

Elsie returned to the cabin full of doughnuts and that warm feeling of *home*. Rose had truly built something amazing for herself. She'd found a loving husband. They were both great parents to their adorable kids, and they were involved in this ranch, which did something important for people who needed it.

That brought her mind to Nate. She thought he was finally starting to take everything more seriously, which was a good first step. Would he have needed this place if people believed him, though?

She shook her head. She couldn't concern herself with what might have happened if things had been different. She couldn't concern herself about *Nate* aside from his function in her mission.

The break to eat breakfast with Rose *had* given Elsie an idea. Revival had all sorts of security systems. Alarms and cameras here and there. She could hack into their system and look at the footage over the past few days to see if anything was out of place.

It'd probably be easier to do with Nate, but even if she thought he should be slightly more concerned about having a hitman after him, she realized him doing everything he normally did was both important to keep *her* cover, and not to give the hitman any idea they knew what might be coming.

But what if it's coming right now? And some innocent person is caught in the crossfire?

Elsie blew out a breath. She remembered Reece telling her once that you had to take a mission step-by-step, because the whole would overwhelm you.

She missed Reece Montgomery. He'd once been a lead field operative and, after her initial discomfort at his quiet, intense ways, she'd appreciated that he was always calm. Sabrina was a ball of energy. Holden was always trying to *charm* someone. But Reece was steady.

Now he was getting married, expecting his first kid, and coaching baseball for his stepson. Like some kind of perfect suburban dad. It *delighted* Elsie to no end. In fact, she'd call him tonight. He did still owe her some candy, and she wanted to know how Henry's latest baseball game had gone.

For now, though, she had to get to work.

She hacked into Revival's system with such ease she gave half a thought to telling Becca she needed to upgrade her system. Maybe Elsie would even offer to do it pro bono... After this mission was complete.

Like she often did, she got lost in what she was doing. Forgot to check the time or to eat a meal. She drank the pop or snacked on the sour candies next to her computer. She watched footage, noted odd comings and goings, and cross-referenced people on the video screen with members of Revival Ranch based on the pictures in their files.

Confidential files. She tried not to pry into anyone's business. Just got a name and a picture, and an idea of what bunk each soldier was in so she could make sure they were where they were supposed to be.

There was one face, however, that popped up now and again that seemed off. A quick search showed the woman was the sister to one of the soldiers, but why would she be walking around the ranch by herself? Most of the guests spent all their time with their family member.

Elsie took some screenshots and was about to do a check through whatever police database she could sneak into without detection when her back door eased open.

Nate slid inside, clearly sneaking around. That was good. She didn't need any more close calls like this morning. Rose could have easily just come inside without knocking and seen...

Well, she wouldn't have seen anything incriminating considering Elsie had been at a table and chairs and Nate had been on the couch, but Elsie would still have had some explaining to do. Explaining that couldn't be covered up by saying she and Nate were...

Her face got hot as Nate frowned at her.

"Don't you have any of those blue ray blocking glasses or whatever?"

"Oh, blue light glasses? I think so. Somewhere." She waved at the counter where she thought she'd left them. She always meant to wear them, but then she got caught up and...

Nate held out the glasses. She blinked up at him. And like this morning when he'd woken and met her gaze, her stomach did that long, slow roll.

It was really kind of nice. Nice enough she forgot herself and just stared at him. Until he jiggled the glasses at her.

Right. She took the glasses and slid them on. "I might have found something. I hacked into Revival's security systems. Just seeing if something was off anytime. Do you recognize this woman?" She pointed at the screen where she'd paused it.

Nate stared at the image. Something went across his face, but she couldn't read it. He stepped back and then frowned at her.

"Justin Sherman's sister."

"Yes. She's one of the few family members who routinely shows up on screen alone. And she shows up a lot."

"She lives just outside of Blue Valley. Her and her husband visit a lot," Nate said.

"So where's her husband?" She pulled up another screenshot of the woman standing outside Nate's bunk. "Where's her brother?" Elsie knew she was on to something. A sister of a soldier seemed a little odd, but there had to be *some* reason this woman was lurking. And with everything going on—

"Listen, I'm going to be scarce for a few days."

Elsie blinked at Nate. Had he just spoken a foreign language? Or maybe received a head injury. "We don't have *a few days*. We have a lead."

He shrugged, as if it didn't matter. "Rumors all over

the place because of last night. Jack was glaring daggers at me. All the guys are ragging on me. Even my therapist brought it up."

"Maybe don't fall asleep on my couch."

"Look, you do your thing. I'll do mine. We'll reconvene in a few days."

"You aren't the boss of me, Nate." She thought he'd finally got it through his thick skull he was in trouble. Or that he could at least trust her. But she knew…he was lying to her. Something else was going on.

"And you aren't the boss of me, Elsie." He gave her an infuriating shrug then left her cabin as if that was that.

She seethed at the closed door. She knew—she *knew*—he was lying to her. He had something up his sleeve, or some new lead to follow, and he was cutting her out.

Oh, no. No, no, no. Nate Averly was working *with* her, whether he liked it or not. That meant she'd need a little muscle to get that across. She grabbed her phone and punched the number for North Star headquarters.

When Shay answered, Elsie grinned at the door. Perhaps a little menacingly. "Shay? I need backup. As soon as you can get it here."

MONICA HADN'T BEEN keen on his leaving Revival right away. She'd also only okayed two days when he might need more.

And would take more. Therapist approved or not.

The next step was lying to his brother. Something Nate didn't relish, but necessary steps were necessary.

He packed the backpack, made sure to mention his absence to a few of the guys—giving Justin Sherman a slightly different story than the rest.

He told Justin the truth.

Because he'd known from the beginning something was off about Justin's sister, and her showing up on Elsie's screen had proved it. He'd let his...discomfort with Courtney's *overtures* keep him far away from the woman.

But Brina had been shot and there were hitmen involved. He had to take the reins and make something happen.

Because no matter how many times he'd told himself for two years he wasn't paranoid, he wasn't suffering delusions from PTSD, there had been a small part of him that had sometimes wondered if he wasn't... just a little crazy.

He shook his head. Didn't matter. In the here and now, he knew what he was doing. And he knew he had to keep Elsie out of it.

She just wasn't...

He paused in his packing, trying to determine what Elsie was or wasn't, but then packed away. Elsie wasn't his problem, and he didn't owe her much of anything. Except maybe thanks she'd showed him that video.

He'd given her the information he had—information she could likely use to prove whatever needed to be proved. But she wasn't the target of this. And shouldn't be.

Nate caught a ride into town with one of the guys headed to Bozeman to pick up the food delivery for the mess hall.

Blue Valley wasn't much. Mostly just a main street with a diner, a bar, a few specialty shops mostly geared to ranching folk, and then, at the end of the street, in a tiny stone building, Blue Valley PD.

Nate walked into the building, which boasted one main room with a jail cell built into the corner. There were two desks—one for the sheriff and one for the dispatcher—and a little door at the back that led to a narrow hall with bathroom and a cot that Nate knew his brother used a lot more often since his wife had taken off last year.

This afternoon, Garrett was at his desk, his dog Barney at his feet, per usual. Garrett's lone dispatcher had made Barney a little scarf with a badge and insisted Barney wear it if he was going to be within the tiny department walls.

Garrett's eyebrows rose when he saw Nate walk in. Barney, fierce guard dog that he was, continued to sleep. Mrs. Linley was on the phone in her corner desk, but she waved at Nate all the same.

"Coming to confess your crimes?" Garrett asked good-naturedly, but there was the way that Garrett looked at him. Always sizing him up, like he could *see* the PTSD on him.

As oldest brother, as police officer for this tiny town, Garrett would never consider that something might not be under his jurisdiction—and therefore not his fault.

"Hey, listen. Monica gave me a few days' leave and I wanted to borrow your fishing cabin." That, at least, wasn't a lie. Garrett had a very isolated fishing cabin, only accessible by boat. Nate would be able to watch for the inevitable ambush.

The genial smile on Garrett's face immediately melted away. "Nate."

"Therapist approved. I'm going to hike over and grab Mom's car. I'll be at your fishing cabin the whole time. Just a little breather."

God, he hoped the ambush was inevitable so he could end this. Far away from anyone who might be caught in the crosshairs.

Elsie's face popped into his mind, but he pushed it away. She might be part of some group, but she was a tiny slip of a thing better suited for sitting in front of computers rather than running real missions.

He could handle this himself.

"Nate…"

"You can keep saying my name in that condescending big-brother way, but Monica okayed it. She said it'd be good for me to have some time to myself."

Garrett's frown didn't dissipate. "I want to search your pack."

It wasn't a surprise. In fact, Nate knew exactly what Garrett would be looking for. He handed the backpack to his brother.

"I'm not going to kill myself, Garrett."

"That's good to hear." But he still checked Nate's bag like Nate was some kind of common criminal. Barney watched the proceedings without lifting his head from his paws.

When Garrett handed the bag back to Nate, he held

Nate's gaze. "I love you. I'm not letting anything happen to you, even if that hurts your feelings."

"I'm not in a bad place. I promise." Nate supposed that was only half a lie. Mentally, he wasn't. But…well, there *could* be someone after him.

That's why he'd left his gun in the flowerpot outside. He knew the way his brother thought.

Garrett opened a drawer and pulled out a keychain. He slid one key off it, but didn't hand it over. "Grab some food before you go. It's not stocked. I haven't been up there in a while, and Dad hasn't, either."

"If I tell Mom I'm headed up there, she'll load me down with food."

"You gonna tell Mom?"

"Yeah. Like I said, it's just a break, Garrett. No need for you guys to worry."

The words Garrett didn't say hung between them. *But we will.*

And that irritated Nate enough to turn the tables on his brother. "Maybe you should be more worried about *you* being in a bad place."

"I'm fine," Garrett said gruffly.

"How many nights you slept on the back cot this week?"

"All of them," Mrs. Linley chimed in from the corner, her hand covering the receiver as she gave Garrett a disapproving look before going back to her conversation.

Barney gave a little growl as he rolled over, like he was agreeing with Mrs. Linley.

"You tell me how much you want to sleep in your

own bed after you find out your wife's been sleeping with someone else in it."

"So burn it. Sell the house. Find something new." Nate shrugged. "Start over, Garrett. It's been a year."

Garrett blinked, because while everyone in the family liked to chime in about Nate's PTSD, the subject of Garrett's wife was always so off-limits. How was that fair?

"Where's your fishing gear?" Garrett asked, clearly changing the subject.

That was fine enough for now. Nate had bigger fish to fry for the time being.

"At Mom and Dad's." Nate held out his hand, waiting for Garrett to finally relinquish the key.

Garrett handed it over, but he was frowning. "I could go with you."

"And leave Blue Valley unmanned? Whatever would the good citizens do when roving bands of criminals come sweeping through?"

"Oh, fine, go," Garrett muttered. "If you're making fun of me and Blue Valley, you can't be that messed up."

Nate held up the key and grinned. "Your faith in me is earth-shattering, Garrett. I'll drop this back off in a few days."

"Forty-eight hours, Nate. Check in every night. With me."

Nate rolled his eyes as Garrett kept calling instructions after him, probably long after Nate had escaped the building and closed the door.

He grabbed his gun, stuck it in his pack. He pretended to be fully absorbed with that, but really he was surveying the town around him. Was someone waiting? Watching? He didn't notice anything out of place, didn't feel any eyes on him.

But the time would come.

He set out on the trek to his parents' ranch and made sure to leave a clear trail.

Step one down. A few more to go.

Chapter Nine

Elsie didn't know how she was going to explain this one to her sisters. So, she simply didn't yet. After Nate had left, she'd done some digging and figured out where he would go if he left the ranch.

She didn't believe for a second he was saying they'd reconvene in a few *days* if he wasn't planning on leaving.

He wouldn't go to his parents' house. It was too much like Revival—a working ranch with people who knew him hanging around. A few days meant he wouldn't go too far, she didn't think.

He'd known that woman on the video, and he'd been suspicious enough to clam up. And if Nate had suspicions... Why wouldn't he tell her?

Did he think she'd been born yesterday? Or was he just that used to doing things on his own because everyone thought he was paranoid?

No. She would *not* feel sorry for him. No, no, no. He knew she believed him. So, regardless of everyone else, he should trust her. Confide in her. She was *trying* to help.

But he was running away. To accomplish something. She understood—deep in her gut—that he was up to something.

That meant, after looking through all his and his family's properties, his brother's isolated fishing cabin was the best candidate. If the woman on the ranch premises—who, for all intents and purposes, had a reason for being at Revival—tipped Nate off to *something*, he was likely getting off Revival to lay some kind of trap.

When Elsie caught movement in her cabin out of the corner of her eye, she didn't even startle. Knowing she'd asked for backup meant knowing a North Star operative might show up like that at any moment.

"You got here fast," she said to the woman in the corner wearing all black—down to a black cap to hide a riot of red hair.

"I was already on my way," Mallory Trevino said, peeling off the wall and walking toward Elsie at her computer. She was one of the newer operatives, but Shay knew Elsie liked working with the women on the team the best. "I've been waiting for you to need some help."

"Well, I need it. Our target thinks he's so smart, but he's about to realize he can't shake me that easily. My theory is he's going somewhere isolated, alone, to try to face down whoever's watching him. I've got a line on the woman it might connect to, but I want to show Nate a thing or two." Elsie pressed a few keys on her keyboard and brought up a map. She pointed to the computer screen. "I think he'll be here. Do you know how to pilot a boat?"

Mallory smirked. "Naturally."

"Gotta love a North Star operative. You didn't come by bike, did you?"

Mallory laughed. "No, I leave the motorcycles in this kind of terrain to Sabrina." She sobered, just a little bit.

"Everyone told me she's going to be okay," Elsie said, trying to smother the little blip of panic and worry.

"Yeah, she is. I just hate that I was sitting around here twiddling my thumbs instead of there with her."

"That's the job. You can't be the one to save everyone. That's why we have a team."

Mal smiled, if sadly. "Yeah, I know. I've got a Jeep a few miles out. Be a bit of a hike, but I didn't want to arouse suspicion."

Elsie nodded. "That'll be good. I'm packed and ready to go. Hike, Jeep, this cabin. I've got it plugged into my phone."

"So, just to be clear… Your plan is to get there first, break into this cabin and lie in wait?" Mallory asked as Elsie shoved her laptop into the backpack she was planning to take along.

"Yes, and hopefully scare the tar out of him in the process so he learns his lesson about lying to me." Elsie still hadn't figured out what she was going to tell Delia and Rose about her absence for a day or two. It depended on how Nate reacted when she caught him red-handed, she supposed.

"Who knew Elsie had a bloodthirsty streak."

"I'm not sure I knew it. Or had one, until I met Nate Averly." She wanted to punch the guy. *Again.*

"Uh-oh."

Elsie looked up at Mallory as she shrugged into the backpack. "Uh-oh what?"

"I mean, you see what's been happening here."

"Where?"

"Since this whole thing started. First Reece," Mallory said, holding up one finger then a second. "Then Holden. Sabrina, too. Though word is Connor's joining North Star rather than Sabrina defecting once she's better."

Elsie laughed, Mallory's meaning dawning on her. Because Reece had fallen for his mission, and then so had Holden. Apparently, Sabrina too. "You can't honestly think…"

Mallory shrugged.

"I'm not an operative."

"But you are a woman. And Nate Averly *is* a man."

"An infuriating one."

"Tell me one thing," Mallory continued as she slid out the back door of the cabin, scanning their surroundings before she started striding for the trees. Elsie followed. "And you can only answer this question with a simple yes or no. No equivocations or explanations. Is he hot?"

"I…"

"Yes or no, Els."

Elsie scowled and hunched her shoulders. "Yes," she muttered. "I'm not attracted to traditionally hot guys, though."

Mallory let out a little hoot of laughter. "Stop, Elsie, we're trying to be stealthy. You can't make me laugh like that."

"Why is that funny?"

"You can't think a guy is *hot* and not be attracted to him."

"Of course you can. I'm being objective about his looks."

"Either you think he's hot or not. You're attracted or you're not. Sure, you don't have to *act* on it, but you better watch yourself. If *Sabrina* can get knocked over by the love stick, even if it was by a former Navy SEAL, who is *definitely* hot by the way, and Holden is besotted with a *farm* girl, and Reece can be taken out by a little blonde with a kid, any of us is vulnerable."

Elsie frowned at Mallory's back. That was all pure silliness. Attraction didn't equal love, and the thing about Reece, Holden and Sabrina was that they *were* formidable. It made sense on both sides—that they'd fallen and the person they'd fallen for had fallen right back. Sure, she could see someone thinking *she* might fall for Nate—the nerdy computer girl and the imposing former Navy SEAL who was wounded in more ways than one.

But the other way around? LOL.

They hiked for a good hour before they made it to Mallory's Jeep—and Elsie knew she was the one who'd made it take that long. Her head pounded and she felt awful. Likely the aftereffects of the drugging, but that didn't mean she could ignore how out of shape she actually was. Maybe she'd start working out once she got back to North Star headquarters.

"You haven't been listening to the doctor's orders, have you?" Mallory asked, eyeing her suspiciously as they got in the Jeep. "Let me guess…little sleep, nothing but junk food."

Elsie pouted but she didn't answer. Because, of course, Mal was right on target.

They headed out, Elsie giving instructions. When they reached the lake, Mallory drove around a little bit to determine the best place to park her Jeep where it wouldn't be easily visible. Once they'd parked and gotten out, they walked toward the rickety dock and even ricketier rowboat.

"This really going to get us across?" Elsie asked, eyeing the watercraft wearily. If they capsized, her laptop would be toast.

"Sure thing. I'll row you over and drop you off at the cabin. I'll row back and then hide in the woods with my Jeep until you give the signal."

Elsie nodded. From shore, she could see the cabin on the little island. The sun shone brightly on the small dot of land and the rough-hewn cabin in the middle. But there was a storm brewing in the distance, and Elsie thought it looked a lot more ominous than charming.

She straightened her shoulders. Hopefully, Nate thought it was charming or relaxing, and then *bam*.

Was he in for the surprise of a lifetime.

It FELT GOOD to row, to be away from the ranch and the men and be *alone*.

The sun was already setting—thanks to the hours he'd had to endure at his parents' house being loaded down with food and advice. The storm clouds in the distance were tinged with a riot of red and orange.

He understood why Garrett came here. It was isolated, but a person didn't feel *alone*. The craggy mountain peaks, the gently lapping water of the mirror-clear lake, that famous big sky above—it all felt like it was teeming with life. A beautiful one at that.

Something Nate didn't have the luxury of thinking about because he wasn't here to rest his soul. He was here to prove that Courtney Prokop was shady as hell.

Nate had spent a lot of time looking into all of them—her brother, her husband, the woman herself. But he'd never been able to unearth anything.

Well, Elsie would work on that and he would work on *action*. Whether it was Courtney herself or a hitman who met him here, it would be an answer. Because, aside from his family, no one else knew this was where he'd been heading.

Except Justin.

About halfway across the lake, Nate knew someone was in the cabin. From his vantage point, he could see the flicker of a light through the curtain of the window. He could see that the mud around the dock had been recently disturbed.

He didn't stop rowing. This was what he'd been working toward. He rowed right for the dock, but took some time to carefully and stealthily take the gun out of his backpack.

He docked, pretending like he didn't have a care in the world, even as he watched every flutter of that curtain. Once on the dock, he drew his gun and kept low to the ground. He tried to scan the banks of the lake, but it was too dark now. Still, he had a feeling someone was out there. Watching. Waiting.

And someone was inside.

He was surrounded.

Maybe you should have trusted someone for help.

He pushed that thought away as a low rumble of thunder echoed across the sky. He could—and *would*—handle this. He inched toward the cabin, watching the shore for some sign of something. Once he reached the door, he could see enough of a swath of light that he realized it wasn't fully latched.

He frowned. What kind of careless criminal was this? Maybe a trap? They thought he was *that* dumb.

Aren't you going to be?

He ignored the voice in his head as he eased the door open, feeling like he was a SEAL again. All those tactics came back to him—without the gear, without the backup.

But there was no team of people to take him out. No spy—or whatever Courtney Prokop was.

There was only Elsie.

She sat there on the floor, legs crossed in front of her, a laptop balanced there. Her hair rioted around her shoulders, and she was wearing the same clothes she'd had on yesterday…because clearly she hadn't done anything except stare at that computer all day.

She yawned, completely unconcerned by the gun pointed at her. "What took you so long?"

Nate was frozen. He didn't even lower the gun. He just stared at her. How… *How?* "What the hell is going on?"

She raised her dark gaze from the computer—apparently dead set on ruining her eyes—and looked at the gun with an air of boredom. "Do you *mind*?"

He lowered the gun, stepped fully in and closed the door behind him. "What are you doing here, Elsie?"

"That was going to be my question for you."

"This is *my* brother's cabin. *I* have every reason to be here. You, on the other hand, do not." How had she figured out he would come here?

She kept staring at him, her gaze even and, if he wasn't mistaken, trying to hide a flare of temper.

His gut should *not* tighten at the sign of a little temper on Elsie Rogers.

"I was sent here to work *with* you, Nate," she said calmly, as if talking to a child having a tantrum. Or a man with PTSD. "Something you seem to have a really hard time getting through your thick skull."

"I didn't ask for your help."

"But you need it."

"I do not. I don't need you here. If I did, I would have asked. How…how the hell did you know I'd come here?"

"You're hardly unpredictable. It was obvious the second you looked at that woman on the screen that you had something up your sleeve. Saying we'd reconvene in a few days? Well, it doesn't take a genius to figure out that means you're going somewhere. I know enough hardheaded former military men who think they can save the world one-handed to make the leap to what your plan would be."

"I don't think you're stupid," he muttered.

"No, I don't think you think beyond your own nose. But you're going to have to. We are a team. Whether you asked, whether you like it or not. That's it. And you can keep trying to sneak off and have a manly showdown, but it's not happening. I will be able to figure out your every move before you make it. So stop making things difficult and work *with* me."

Elsie did not get up. She did not move the computer off her lap. She looked more like a waif than even a computer nerd, but the haughty, almost regal look she directed at him gave her the aura of someone very much in charge.

He was about to tell her she needed to get over the idea she would ever be in charge of *him*, but something outside the door moved. He whirled, gun aimed, ready to shoot the intruder just as Elsie let out a heavy sigh.

"Relax. She's with me."

"Of course she is," Nate muttered, dropping his gun arm as a woman appeared seemingly out of thin air. "Why wouldn't she be?"

The woman grinned at him. But when she turned to Elsie, her expression went serious. "Someone is out there. I can't tell if they're just watching or if they're planning on coming out here. I didn't think I should wait around to find out."

"Good call. Mallory, this is Nate. Nate, this is Mallory."

"Hey," she said with a nod. "Got anything, Els?"

"Not yet. Do you think if I got the camera on the Jeep up and running, we'd be able to get an ID?"

The woman dressed in black—Mallory—seemed to give this some thought.

"There's no reason to get an ID. I know who it is, or who sent them, anyway."

"The woman on the video," Elsie said, her voice was cool. Detached. Like she was *mad* at him.

Why did that make him feel bad? He'd made the right choice. Even if she'd figured him out. It was the *right* choice and her and her friend needed to get the hell out of here.

"I have never been able to figure out what the Prokops have to do with this, but I know they—or at least Courtney—does."

"Ah, so you suspected they had *something* to do with it and didn't think to tell me? Interesting."

The accusation made him defensive even though she was right. "You knew who she was. You decided she was shady all on your own. I figured you'd research that."

"While you went off and played hero?"

"While I went off and ended my yearslong nightmare, Elsie."

"Well," Mallory said, studying him and then Elsie, "I'm going to go watch the actual threat while you guys argue. Cool?"

She wasn't asking him. Elsie nodded and Mallory slipped back out again.

"Are you…in charge?"

She snorted. "Hardly." She frowned a little. "Well, lead operative on this mission, I guess. Anyway. That's not important. You being thoughtless and a liar isn't important, either."

"Hey—"

"What's important is figuring out what this random woman has to do with a military cover-up. I looked up her brother…this Justin Sherman. He was in the Army. So, presumably, had no connection to you and the SEALs."

"As far as I can tell."

"I know families are all different, but Courtney and Don uprooted their whole lives to come live in Blue Valley when her brother got accepted to Revival." Elsie frowned at her screen. "Maybe it's less about the branch of military, the connection to you, and more about the timing. Once you were discharged from the hospital, you came home to your parents' ranch."

She typed some things, and Nate found he didn't particularly care for how much she knew about him. Down to *dates*.

"A year later, you join Revival. A month after that, Justin joins. It's not totally suspect timing, but… I need to get into applications and when those went through. Oh, and maybe Justin's military references. Yeah, and…"

"How do you have all that information?" Nate demanded.

She looked at him over the laptop. Her eyes were a little blurry, but she blinked and they sharpened.

Because she was still mad at him. Clearly.

"I could get all sorts of information on you, Nate," she said with the wave of a hand. "I could read your therapy records if I really wanted to. Luckily, I have a code of ethics I'll only break if someone is in mortal danger. I'll only hack into the information I actually need to do my job."

"I don't have anything to hide."

"Except Courtney Prokop."

She turned the laptop toward him. It was another security video. But instead of Courtney sneaking around outside, it was her following Nate into his bunk.

Nate winced. "That's not…what it looks like."

"Oh, and what does it look like, Nate?" Elsie asked, all faux innocence.

Nate was saved by Mallory, because she stuck her head in the door. "We got one in a boat coming."

Elsie nodded at Mallory, but that did not work for Nate on any level. "You get her out of here," he said to Mallory. "I'll take care of this."

Chapter Ten

Elsie laughed. She should probably be more offended, but Nate trying to boss around a North Star operative *was* hilarious.

Mallory smiled at Elsie. "Is this guy serious?"

"I think so. You'll have to forgive him. He's not used to people helping him out."

"Pro tip—don't order people around. They don't like it. And I don't take orders from you. You two stay here. I'm going to watch his approach. If I can incapacitate him without help, I will. If I need backup, I'll whistle."

"No. Absolutely not. You two will stay here—"

"Is this because I'm a woman?" Mallory returned, crossing her arms over her chest and serving Nate a killing look.

Elsie watched frustration chase confusion on Nate's face. But he shook his head and kept digging the hole deeper.

"I don't care if you're an extraterrestrial—this is *my* deal," he said, jabbing his thumb into his own chest. "My problem. My threat. *I've* been dealing with it—

alone, I might point out—for two years. I didn't ask for you two to crash *my* problem."

Elsie sobered, because there it was again. She felt for him. She was sure he meant well, in a strange sort of way. Maybe he simply didn't know how to let go of all those guards he'd built around himself when no one believed him.

No one. Not even his own brother. She honestly couldn't imagine what that might be like. Because, no matter what, she'd always had her sisters.

Nate didn't know how to be part of a team since his discharge from the military and felt betrayed. He didn't know how to trust. And that gave her an idea.

"We could bring Connor in, if that would make you feel better about help."

Nate's gaze turned from Mallory to her. His eyebrows drew together. "You… What?"

"It'd take probably a day at least to work out, and he'd have to be willing, but we can make it happen. Connor worked with Sabrina. He was integral in taking Daria down. He's capable of handling whatever this is. If it would help for you to have someone you trust here, we can make it happen."

Nate looked at Mallory then back at her. Confusion etched all over his face. "I don't understand."

"We're working with you, Nate. That's the point of us. To work with you, to help you, to figure out who is behind these hitmen…and whatever else is going on. Because, clearly, there's more going on than we know. You're a hitman target, so Mallory's job is to protect you. Sure, I get why that might be a little hard to swallow, and that's fine. We'll find a way to help you swallow it. Now, *my* job is to get to the bottom of this, and while you've been actively working against me, my hope is you'll get to a point where you stop."

Nate rubbed his hand across his jaw. Conflicted. Lost. It took a lot of willpower, and probably Mallory's presence, to keep Elsie seated rather than crossing to him and offering him some physical comfort.

A totally friendly physical comfort. Totally.

"Let's take this one step at a time," Elsie said gently. "The threat currently. You said someone's in a boat, Mal?"

"Yeah. One guy. Heavily armed. Might be the hitman."

Elsie nodded. "Okay. For right now, we'll go with Mallory's plan. She takes care of the guy. If she needs backup from you, Nate, she'll whistle."

Before Nate could argue—and Elsie had no doubt he'd been planning to argue—Mallory slipped back out into the night surrounding the cabin.

Elsie took a deep breath, to center herself and keep the calm. She gripped her laptop maybe a little tightly because the computer was her security blanket. She didn't relish being in charge, but she would have to be until Nate really let himself be part of their team. "Now, we can talk about bringing Connor in."

"I don't want Connor mixed up in this any more than he already is."

Elsie nodded. She should have known his hard head wouldn't just accept the easiest answer. She set the laptop aside and got to her feet. It made her feel exposed, but this really wasn't about her and her feelings.

She stood in front of Nate, met his gaze and tried to find words that would get through all that…hurt. He'd been hurt. For years. By people he'd trusted.

She knew that was the kind of thing you didn't get over just because someone told you to. But she had to try.

"Look. I need you to really absorb this, and I'd love to give you time—but I keep telling you, we don't have it. Dude in a boat with a gun out there. You are part of a *team*, Nate. You have to let people in. Lean on people and let them lean on you. We all want the same result. All of us. And we're here to *help*. The thing about help is, you have to accept it. You have to work with it. Or instead of working against the bad guy, we're all working against each other."

He looked at someplace on the wall beyond her, big arms crossed over his chest. "I don't want anyone in danger."

"We're already here. Mal and I? We've been in plenty of dangerous situations. It's our job. A job we both love. It isn't a duty. No one is forcing us to be here. We chose this job, this group, this work. You didn't. I get that. But *we* did."

His dark eyes met her earnest gaze. "Why?" he asked, baffled.

"I'm sure a wide variety of reasons."

"I don't mean them. I mean you. Why would you put yourself in harm's way after…?"

She shrugged, uncomfortable that everything seemed to keep going back to her bad childhood. Still, she held eye contact, because she knew he needed to believe her.

See that she meant everything she said. "Everyone has a little harm's way in their life, Nate. You can't avoid it. Especially as a woman in the world. But this way? I'm in charge of it. I'm helping people get out of it. It gives me all those choices I didn't have as a kid. And it lets me give those choices to other people who are stuck. You have *choices*, Nate."

"Choices?" he repeated.

"Yes." She didn't fully think the movement through. It was too instinctual. She reached out and grabbed his forearms crossed over his chest. She squeezed. "And you'll have more when this is over. We can help make this over, faster, and with you safer. But you have to trust me. You can't run off. You can't argue with us. You can't cut us all out. Trust us. Please. If not all of us, at least me."

"It's not that I don't trust you."

"Well, start acting like it, then."

"It's…hard."

"I know." She should pull her hands away. She should focus on the impending danger. She should do anything over this getting all soft and mushy about him. But he seemed so lost and…and… "I know." And she just… stood there. Stupidly. Looking up at him. Words lost in that dark, direct gaze.

He wasn't looking at her any special way. He was thinking. About hitmen and Connor. If it *looked* like his gaze was on her mouth, she was clearly having some kind of delusion. But the delusion came with a kind of longing she didn't know what to do with.

A gunshot rang out, followed by the sound of something breaking.

Nate jerked, stumbled forward and swore as a bloom of red appeared on his shirt.

NATE LET THE stream of curse words fall out of him. The pain in his arm was sharp and hot, but bearable. No other shots followed.

He realized, once he was done swearing, that Elsie was babbling a mile a minute.

"You're bleeding. You're shot. You're… Mal. No. I…"

"It's just my arm, and it's not that bad. Take a breath, Els."

She did so. Immediately. "You've been shot. We have to…" She swallowed, took a long, deep breath and then slowly let it out. "Okay. We're going to bandage you up." She walked stiffly to her pack and pulled out a little first-aid kit.

He doubted a Band-Aid was going to fix this problem, but he had to think. The shot had blasted through the cabin wall. There wasn't a window there, and it was dark, so it was unlikely the bullet had been meant for him.

But that meant Mallory was out there being shot at. Or had already been shot since she hadn't whistled.

Elsie took his arm and studied the wound. In the weak beam of her lantern, she looked pale. Worried. But her hands didn't shake. She'd pulled herself together.

Because she was part of a team on a mission. She'd seen danger and perhaps gunshots before. No matter how slight or pale, little Elsie Rogers wasn't *new* to this.

A team. The last time he'd thought he'd been part of a team, he'd been injured and dishonorably discharged—all for trying to do the right thing.

She put a bandage over the bloody wound, but he knew it wouldn't do much to stop the bleeding. He didn't have time to worry about it. "You stay put." He already had his gun out, so he started for the door.

"You can't go out there!" She grabbed his arm—the one that had been nicked by the bullet—but immediately dropped it when he hissed out a breath of pain.

"That hitman wants you dead, Nate," she said, stepping in front of the door.

"And what do you think Mallory is doing out there? Having a picnic? I have to go help her. Unless you want your friend to die?"

She was wide-eyed and shook her head.

"Let me go. Stay put. Do you have a gun? Do you know how to use a gun?"

She scurried over to where she'd left her computer and picked up a small pistol. Nate didn't have time to frown at the puny weapon. "Keep it loaded and ready to shoot. Anyone who's not me or someone in your group, shoot. No questions asked. Got it?"

She nodded, holding the gun in a death grip. If he wasn't in immediate danger, it might have been funny. Elsie talked a good game about being some operative who knew how to deal with danger, but one gunshot had sure changed her tune.

"Stay put. I mean it," he said and then slid out into the night. Frogs and insects were making their evening noises. The storm hadn't started yet, but flashes of lightning in the distance illuminated the world around him in intervals.

He saw the second boat drifting back toward the center of the lake, unmanned. Whoever had rowed over hadn't secured it. Hadn't had time?

He walked silently around the perimeter of the cabin. He heard a rustle in the trees—sounding a little too loud to be animal. He moved toward it, seeing a light deeper in the trees. His military training had already kicked in, and it was easy to fall back into those old habits. The awareness was still there, the calm that settled over him when he accepted his only goal was to keep himself alive.

He stopped short when he realized what the sight before him was.

Mallory had a penlight in her mouth and was tying a very large man's hands behind his back—and then to another man's hands.

Nate blinked at the two unconscious men tied together. "What—"

"Sorry," she said around the penlight. Once she'd secured the knot, she dropped the light into her hand. "There was someone else here besides Boat Guy. He jumped me before Boat Guy landed. Fought him off, but then Boat Guy came around and we struggled with his gun. Went off in the struggle. Luckily not at me."

"There was someone besides Boat Guy?" Nate's eyes immediately went to the little island's cluster of trees. It hadn't occurred to him someone besides Elsie had beaten him here.

"Yeah. Came from the trees. My guess is he'd been

there for a while." Mallory rolled her shoulders and swore. "Gonna be sore tomorrow." She pointed her penlight at him. "You're bleeding."

"Yeah, bullet nicked me."

"Hell. This is a mess. You go get more than a Band-Aid. I'm calling my boss. I think we need more men on the ground here before we search the island."

Nate hesitated. More men. This secret group. Everything was getting out of control. Out of his hands. He wouldn't know all the moving parts and, in his experience, being in the dark meant you ended up getting the short end of the stick.

"Look, I don't know you and you don't know me," Mal said, stepping over the defeated men and toward Nate. "But I know Elsie. She's the real deal. If you can't trust all of us, you can at least trust her. She trusts you, wants to help you—so I'll do the same. But we need it from you, too."

"Yeah, I…" He didn't know how to do this, but he knew he had to. What's more, he knew Elsie wanted him to. And, for whatever reason, that made him want to and…

Hell. "If Connor doesn't mind, it'd help if he was one of those men."

Mallory nodded. "Let's get back to Elsie and see what we can do."

Chapter Eleven

Elsie hadn't handled that very well, she knew. Even now, her palms were sweaty as she held the gun pointed at the door.

She didn't like guns. Shay had insisted she learn how to shoot one, along with basic self-defense and a few other field operative–type things. Elsie knew she could shoot it, and with good enough accuracy if she was calm enough.

Didn't mean Elsie *liked* it. Or the fact Mallory and Nate were out there with a hitman and she was sitting here, sweating like a…weakling.

She was not meant for the field. Last time she'd been outside headquarters, she'd been drugged and all she'd been doing was sitting in a bunker trying to hack a computer. Now, Nate had been shot and she was just sitting around waiting for everyone else to take care of things.

Because she was *not* a field operative. She was a computer genius. How could Shay have put her in this situation?

How are you going to disappoint Shay in this situation?

Voices were getting closer, and Elsie swallowed and

tried to listen over the heavy pounding of her heart. Relief swelled through her when she finally realized it was Mallory's and Nate's voices. They were the ones who opened and came in through the door. *Thank God.*

She immediately turned the safety on, put the gun down and got to her feet. "Are you guys okay?"

"All good. Took down two guys—tied up out there." Mallory nodded toward the door. "I called Shay," Mallory said as she closed the door behind Nate. "She's sending a few more operatives, including Connor, but they won't be here till morning."

"Do we stay?"

"I think so. Not sure if there's more here, but it's a good place to hunker down and watch for any more threats. Nate and I will take turns watching out, so we can each get some sleep. Rain's starting, so hopefully that keeps everyone laying low."

Elsie stepped forward then stopped because she just felt…superfluous. Still, she pointed to his arm. "Nate, you need better…"

"I've got some field dressing in my pack." Mallory was already digging stuff out and taking off the silly bandage Elsie had put on his serious wound. She took care of it and, while she did, she and Nate talked in low tones about everything that had happened outside the cabin.

They did not include her in the conversation. Elsie knew it wasn't fair to feel hurt. They'd done the hard work. *They* knew how to deal with guns and threats.

They were…in charge. Doing things. Leaning into their strengths. She couldn't be a field operative. She didn't know how to be a soldier or a spy. She could let all she didn't know or couldn't do overwhelm her.

Or she could remember there were things she *did* know. That she *did* have a function here and that it was time to stop worrying about guns and bandages and *do it*.

She was here for a reason. Maybe a large portion of that was her family ties—but she wouldn't let that be the *only* reason. She grabbed her phone and marched for the door.

"Elsie." Nate tried to stop her from opening the door, but she shook him off. She walked into the dark and went to where the men were tied together, starting to come to. Thunder rolled, lightning flashed, and she got progressively wet as she walked. Still, she pulled out her phone.

"Say cheese, boys." She took one picture, the bright light of the flash making them wince, then the next while Nate watched her. Speechless apparently. When she turned back to the cabin, he gaped at her.

"What are you *doing*?" Nate demanded.

"What I'm damn good at," Elsie said, back to feeling in control. "Pull them inside. We're going to figure out who they are." And by *we* she meant *me*.

Nate and Mal worked together to drag the men into the cabin. Only one was fully conscious and fighting his bonds. They were all soggy puddles by the time it was done, but Elsie hardly noticed.

She'd settled in with her computer, ignoring the men, ignoring Nate and Mallory. She uploaded the pictures and began her search.

"You don't have to look this one up," Nate said,

scowling at the bald guy who was still unconscious. "That's Don Prokop."

Elsie's eyebrows rose, but she didn't look at Nate. She kept her eyes on her computer. Just because they knew who he was didn't mean there wasn't more to know.

"He was the one waiting in the trees," Mallory said. "Other one's the hitman."

"Funny." Elsie typed a few things in and it took her less than a minute to find what she was looking for on the first guy. "That's not the only name Don goes by, FYI. He has at least two aliases, and rap sheets for both."

"Well, that's new information," Nate said.

"We'll look deeper into these other names soon, and who else they might connect to, but first let's figure out contestant number two." She typed and searched. This man had come to, and while he didn't fight his bonds anymore, his eyes were full of fury, like he was just biding his time.

His picture was proving trickier to connect to an identity, but that only convinced Elsie his identity was important.

"Good luck, little girl," he growled.

Elsie raised an eyebrow at him then pushed a few more keys. Dug past a few fake names with ease. She knew exactly what to look for. And how. "You like a fake name, don't you?" she asked cheerfully. "But Lee Braun is the real one, huh?"

The angry expression on the man's face slackened into shock.

Elsie smiled sweetly at the criminal. "I'll take that as a yes."

NATE COULDN'T SAY he had time to *reel* exactly, but watching Elsie go from shaking mess over a flesh wound to in-charge snark queen was…well, it left a man a little off-kilter.

It certainly left Lee Braun, hitman, off-kilter. The man looked like he'd been dealt a blow by a two-by-four instead of some information unearthed by a computer fairy.

"That was enjoyable to watch," Nate managed to say. Elsie turned her smile up to him.

"It was enjoyable to do, too." She was so *pleased* with herself, he couldn't help but smile back. She had the faintest little dimple in her cheek when she smiled and…

Mallory cleared her throat.

Elsie blinked and turned her attention back to the computer, a blush creeping up her cheeks. But when she spoke, her voice was easy and even.

He was sure his would have sounded perfectly strangled.

"Now. I'll need some time to a do a little deep dive. What are we going to do with these guys? They need to be detained. We could get local law enforcement to pick up Don on any number of these charges. Based on his record, he's not much of a threat. Definitely not the brains of the operation."

Dread leaped into Nate's gut at the words *local law enforcement*. Luckily that dread was much preferable to the complicated, uncomfortable thing twisting his gut when he'd shared a smile with Elsie. "Let's not… do that," Nate managed to mutter.

"Oh, too late on that," Mallory offered. "Shay already delegated cleanup. That means she'll likely come to the same conclusion Elsie did and send locals."

"You can't send locals. You can't…"

Mallory looked at him like he'd lost it. "They can handle Don. He's a nobody. We'll keep the hitman and—"

"Call this Shay back and tell her no. Or she can call Valley County. You don't want Blue Valley. Small PD. Just one guy."

"You got a history with this one guy?" Mallory asked suspiciously.

"You could say that."

"It's his brother," Elsie supplied, though she seemed like she wasn't paying too close attention to them. She was tapping away. Face far too close to the computer. The woman needed to get outdoors and stop staring at a screen all the time. She was going to be blind by the time she was forty.

And she needed to stop rattling off things he didn't really want to tell Mallory or anyone.

"So, let's keep him out of it," Nate said firmly. "For his own good." And for Nate's. If Garrett saw Nate was hurt…

"It's already been done," Mallory replied with a shrug. "Whoever Shay was going to call to pick him up has already been called. No undoing it."

Nate didn't groan, though he wanted to. What would his brother be thinking if he got a call for the fishing cabin? He was probably worst-case scenario-ing everything. And Nate *had* been shot.

"You really can't expect a one-man department to handle this guy. They barely have a real jail. They—"

"Nate, relax. Whoever Shay called, she knew what she was doing. A smaller department is actually better, because it allows us to bend some rules. I'm sure Garrett can handle it, if she did indeed call Garrett."

Nate didn't argue more. It was clearly pointless. His arm throbbed, but that was the least of his worries. Garrett. Here. How was he going to explain…any of this?

And how had he gotten to the point where he'd been shot, and had absolutely no control? When this had been his entire world for two years, and no one had come after him or hurt him or…

"You should go wait for whoever is coming on the banks, on the off chance there are more men here. We don't want locals ambushed," Elsie said, looking pointedly at Mallory and nodding toward Nate.

"What about these guys?" Nate asked, eyeing the two large, dangerous men in the cabin.

"They're tied up and incapacitated. Besides, I'm going to enjoy telling Lee all the information I'm finding out about him."

She was just bound and determined to get herself hurt. Bound and determined to complicate this thing. If she'd left him alone, he could have handled Don and the hitman. He could have handled everything. On his own, and…

Well, he might have been able to incapacitate the two men after him. But then what? He didn't have any mysterious group or computer skills to figure out Don's aliases or Lee Braun's identity. He didn't have anyone—

except Garrett—to handle the two men. And that would have been only if he'd gotten Garrett to believe him.

So, he had to accept, no mater how hard it was, that he needed Elsie and Mallory and their group. To *really* finish things. Not just to prove he was right, but to stop whoever was after him from hurting more people.

It was the strangest, most out-of-body realization he'd had in his life—and he'd had a *lot* of those in the past few years.

He *needed* these women and their associates.

He shook his head. Need didn't mean he'd allow Elsie to get hurt in the process. Nate picked up the gun she'd put down the minute they'd walked in and placed it next to her on the table. "Use that if you need to."

She wrinkled her nose, but she nodded.

Nate followed Mallory out, looking at the tied-up men as he left. Don was still unconscious. Lee was glaring at Elsie. Nate didn't like it, but he didn't like *any* of this.

They moved to the bank. He could hear the soft sound of a motorboat rather than a rower.

"He moves fast."

Nate grunted. Garrett would take any call seriously, but Nate knew one that potentially involved him would in fact get Garrett to break land and speed records to be there. "You should have let me handle this," Nate muttered.

"Sorry, I wasn't informed your brother was law enforcement."

"It wouldn't have mattered if you had been. You'd still have done it."

Mallory chuckled. "You're right." She had her gun drawn, and her gaze kept sweeping the world around them. The rain had let up, but thunder still boomed like another patch of showers might move through. "You sure that's him?" she asked as the boat got close enough to make out most of his features, aided by the flashlight Garrett had strapped to his chest.

"Yeah, that's my brother."

Garrett motored the boat—God only knew where he'd gotten that motorboat since they weren't legal on this lake—to the dock and then exited with ease. He started right for them. Mallory let out a low whistle. "What's in the water in Montana?" Then she winked at Nate before sauntering back into the cabin.

"You're okay," Garrett said, standing with his arms crossed over his chest. His badge glinted in the flashlight beam like this permanent wall between them. Garrett had been made to be a cop: that strong sense of right and wrong with a core of fairness and an understanding that justice and the law didn't always go hand in hand. That was why he'd managed to work toward his own Blue Valley department.

Nate, on the other hand, had gotten out. He'd joined the military because it sounded like an adventure, not because he had any special desire to help people. But he *had* helped people. He'd done good things.

Until he'd had to come home and then he'd done… He blew out a breath. He'd been right. All this time he'd been occasionally worried that Garrett and his parents and Monica were right about his mental state, but Elsie had proved… Nate was actually right.

Now they had to do something about it. Nate hadn't wanted Garrett as part of this fight, but here he was.

"Nate," Garrett said darkly as they stood in the night, the lake lapping around them. Anyone could be watching, waiting, but Nate felt rooted to this spot where his brother stood before him like some kind of shining beacon of what was *right* while all Nate felt was wrong.

"Yeah, I'm okay. Where's Barney?" It was an inane question. Nate didn't know what else to say. There was no conversation he wanted to have right now. Might as well talk about his brother's dog.

"Nate. What is going on?" Garrett looked at the cabin. "And who on earth was that woman? Is that why you're… Are you mixed up with this shady character?"

"Not exactly. Not…" Nate trailed off as Elsie came out of the cabin. She had her hands clasped together and Nate could see even in the faint light of the lantern she held there was a tension about her that hadn't been there before.

"Is that…?"

Elsie stopped in front of Garrett, next to Nate. "Hi, Deputy Averly. Sheriff now, Nate said."

"You're one of the Rogers…" Nate watched Garrett very carefully swallow the world *girls*. "Elsie, right?"

"Yes." She smiled. "I'm afraid we're in need of your help. I could make up a very complicated story about how or why, but I think since Nate is deeply involved in this, it might be one of those rare cases where the truth is necessary."

"I have no idea what you're talking about."

"Come inside. We'll get it all hashed out."

Nate wasn't sure any of this would ever be *hashed out*, but he followed Garrett and Elsie into the fishing cabin, which was definitely not built for four people let alone six. Elsie sat with her computer—she'd moved from the floor to the kitchen area with its small table and two chairs. Mallory stood next to the door, watching the world outside the window, and Nate stood in the middle of it all feeling like he was in an alternate universe as Elsie explained everything to Garrett.

Everything. That she was with a secret group. That Nate had uncovered a massive military cover-up. About Brina and Connor and the whole shebang.

Garrett sat there, taking it all in. When Elsie finally stopped giving him details, he shook his head in silence for a good full minute before speaking.

"I'm sorry. I just don't..." Garrett dragged a hand over his face. "This is for real."

"I've been telling you," Nate muttered. His brother's shocked acceptance didn't make him feel any better or vindicated. It made him uncomfortable.

He knew his brother had never *meant* to hurt him with his distrust, so he'd never had any dreams about proving them all wrong. He'd only wanted to...prove it to himself. To end the threat and then move on.

Now Garrett was looking at him like someone had kicked a puppy in front of him.

"Look, we can deal with all that later. Right now, we need you to take care of Don Prokop. Right?" Nate looked at Elsie.

She nodded. "What we need is for you to keep him in a cell for a few days, and make sure no one comes for him. We'll set you up with communications with one of our people at headquarters, so you can contact them if someone does come for him. We can also set you up with some security, so you're more protected."

"And this will help Nate prove…all the things he's been trying to prove?" Garrett asked, eyebrows drawn together, forehead wrinkled.

Elsie nodded. "Yes. And it will help stop this group who's been smuggling guns and sending out hitmen and who knows what all else."

"All right." Garrett raked his hands through his hair and shook his head. "But the unconscious one needs medical attention first. As does my brother."

"I'm fine. All patched up," Nate said, moving his injured arm even though jostling it hurt. Garrett frowned, but at least seemed to believe him. Nate looked over at the two women.

Elsie exchanged a look with Mallory. They seemed to have a whole nonverbal language going on.

"Okay, I'll take Don back to the station with you," Mallory said. "We've got doctors on our staff. We'll do a video conference and one of them will talk us through the medical procedures. One of our tech guys will talk me through figuring out the security situation. Good?"

Garrett looked up at Nate, clearly overwhelmed and lost. But he gave a firm nod. "Good."

Chapter Twelve

Elsie had never shared a small cabin with two fuming men—one of whom was an incapacitated hitman who wanted the other one dead. And the other one was…

Well, a problem. One she didn't have the time to think about.

She had to email directions to one of her tech operatives to set everything up for the Blue Valley PD. She had to field a call from Shay, updating her on their progress, while Shay gave her an ETA for the two operatives she was sending to take care of the hitman. All while she was searching names and delegating certain tasks to her remote tech team.

After Mallory and Garrett had left, Nate had positioned himself by the window, looking out into the night. He held his gun pointed at the man now handcuffed and tied up on the floor.

Nate was angry, certainly. The scowl told Elsie that—no deep analysis necessary. But she knew underneath that anger he was worried. About his brother. About Connor. And, she thought because she was starting to understand him, about what came next.

He acted like his wound was no big deal, and perhaps it wasn't. He'd been a Navy SEAL. Maybe getting shot in the arm was routine for him. And Mallory *had* wrapped him up with something far more effective than a Band-Aid.

That didn't mean he shouldn't take care of himself, though. She got up from her computer and pulled a snack from her pack. She walked over and stood next to him by the window. "You should eat something."

Nate grunted as he took the granola bar she handed him. She stood there while he unwrapped it and took a grudging bite. "This has chocolate chips in it," he said around a mouthful of food.

"Well, of course it does. Who wants to eat plain granola?"

He swallowed. And then handed the bar back to her. "You have a problem, Elsie."

"I have a sweet tooth. It's hardly a problem." She shrugged and ate the bar herself. She looked out at the black outside the window. She should be at her computer, searching. Doing the work she was good at, but she thought Nate needed some conversation.

Or maybe she did. "What do you think happens next?"

"I don't know. I don't understand what's happening now." He glanced at the hitman. "What did you find out on him?"

"As far as I can tell, he doesn't have any ties to the group that wants you dead—if it's a group, which makes sense. If a hitman doesn't have ties, aside from the money he's paid, it can't be traced back to whoever hired him." But she had found someone who *did* have ties and whose husband being mixed up in this made things all the more suspicious.

She found herself really not wanting to broach the topic. But that was weak. And foolish. "What about this Courtney Prokop?"

"What about her?"

He wasn't defensive exactly, but Elsie knew what she'd seen on that security footage and... Well, it was possible Nate had been taken in by the woman. Maybe he'd told her things he shouldn't have when they'd done...whatever they'd done in that cabin. Elsie supposed it didn't matter what he'd done with Courtney. That was over. But it would help if they all knew what exactly had gone on, and she definitely needed him to know Courtney was shady.

It wasn't *personal* interest. It was necessary. "Courtney has ties."

"To what?" Nate demanded, his gaze whipping to her.

Elsie didn't flinch. While the crackling anger in him might usually make her nervous, she *was* used to people being none too pleased about the information she found in the course of a mission.

"She has ties to the military, which wouldn't be a big deal on its own. Lots of people have enlisted or done work for the military. But, connected to everything else going on and how much it's hidden in her records? I have questions. I have a few of my tech people digging deeper since I was focusing on our hitman, so they're sending me reports as they find things. We'll need to study everything more comprehensively, but—"

"I didn't sleep with her," Nate grumbled, looking back out the window. His expression was tense, all hard lines and angles. She wished she could put her hand on his face, somehow soften all that tension inside of him.

And she really had to stop being so soft-hearted. "It's none of my business."

"Well, I didn't. Not for her lack of trying."

Elsie rolled her eyes. "Don't put too fine a point on it, Nate. I'll believe you didn't sleep with her if you really need me to."

He gaped at her, which Elsie had to admit she enjoyed. That she could surprise him into gaping and sputtering. When he finally got a word out, it was a little bit outraged.

"She *did* try. You don't have to believe me, or can think I'm being conceited, but I know what went on in that cabin."

"*Not* sleeping together," Elsie replied, trying and failing to keep her voice from sounding sarcastic.

"Among a million other reasons I didn't sleep with her, she's *married*."

"I'm actually not so sure about that."

Nate's expression kept turning more and more incredulous. "What?"

Elsie blew out a breath and nodded at the hitman in the corner. "Maybe we should talk about this later."

Nate reached out and took her arm, pulling her toward the door. It was a simple touch, his fingers curling around her forearm. It should *not* send a buzz through her skin like she was suddenly all jangling nerves and...

And it was *not* the time or place for those sensations, she reminded herself.

"Explain," he ordered once they were outside. The night had cooled considerably since the storm, but Elsie only felt heat where his hand was wrapped around her arm. He'd situated them so he could look through the window to where their prisoner sat. He kept his gaze on the man, but Elsie knew she had his full attention.

She also knew he held her with his injured arm so she could escape his grasp easily enough if she wanted to. She was sure she should want to.

But she didn't.

"Courtney and Don are definitely connected, but there's no record of any marriage. Nothing legal binding them together."

Nate's grip loosened, though he didn't take his hand off her arm. "I guess it doesn't really matter, does it?"

"Yes and no. The thing is, if you're dealing with people in a secret group, or people working together to do bad things, it's not going to be easy to find actual physical evidence you could use against them in a court of law. But I can find clues, connections and hints that lead us to the people or group, or what have you. Her not being married to Don but using his last name is a clue. A hint."

"To what?"

"Well, I started looking into her maiden name. Unlike him, she doesn't have any aliases—at least that I've found, and I'm very good at finding those. But she has a bank account under that maiden name still. I've got my team following that money right now. Money that seems to have military strings. Maybe she just worked in the military, but we need to know for sure. Obviously, if she were trying to be really sneaky, she'd choose a completely different name, but I'm having my team look into if a Courtney Loren pops up anywhere else. A connection to you or Connor or Daria, or any of the places you guys were stationed, et cetera, et cetera."

"Wait." Nate's grasp on her arm tightened as he seemed to work through everything she'd just said. "Loren? Isn't her maiden name Sherman? Like Justin?"

"No. I checked into that. They have the same mother, but different fathers. Courtney's maiden name is Loren. L-o-r-e-n."

"I..." Nate looked like he'd seen a ghost before he shook his head. He dropped her arm, even took a slight step away from her. "Surely that's a coincidence," he said, more to himself than to her.

"What is?"

"Garrett's ex-wife. Her maiden name was Loren. But..." Nate scraped his free hand through his hair, making it a little wild. "Elsie. Good God."

"First name?"

"Savannah, but it's not poss—"

Elsie hurried into the cabin without waiting for Nate to finish. Could this connect to Garrett? Could Garrett himself be involved? Immersed in discrediting his brother? Wouldn't that make a horrible kind of sense?

She had to find out ASAP. Mallory was *with* Garrett and a man who'd tried to take her out. Elsie hadn't even watched the boat to make sure it had crossed. Mal could take care of herself, of course, but…how would Elsie feel if she'd sent Mallory off with a *dirty* cop?

Elsie's stomach roiled. Rose and Delia might have hated every Valley County sheriff's deputy from their childhood, but Elsie had always tried to keep an open mind. And she'd known Garrett had tried to help. She'd never hated him, or thought he'd done anything wrong.

Was she that off base? Could he be a traitor to his brother and his badge and everything else?

She began to type on her keyboard. She was going to find out. ASAP.

Nate felt a bit like he'd been gonged. He vibrated with an energy he had no outlet for, and his brain buzzed with thoughts he couldn't seem to follow to completion.

The only reason his brain was tethered to consciousness at all was the hitman inside the cabin. There was no way he was leaving Elise alone with him, so he followed close on her heels.

But that didn't mean he understood anything else. He stood in the doorway and looked at her. She sat at the tiny table, already hunched over her computer, tapping away while her dark hair curtained most of her face. She looked like some kind of feral creature, and he had no idea why that was charming.

But he certainly didn't have time to be *charmed*.

This name thing had to be a strange coincidence. It *had* to be. How could Savannah be wrapped up in this? In military stuff? And neither he nor Garrett had ever known?

It wasn't possible. He hadn't liked the woman who'd married his brother, but surely she wasn't… Nate rubbed a hand over his face. He couldn't let his brain go bounding forward. They had to deal with this one step at a time.

The first step was Elsie doing her search. They'd go from whatever information she found.

He moved to stand next to her. When he caught sight of what Elsie was typing on the computer, he forgot everything else.

"What are you doing? Search the ex-wife not…" He stopped because as little as the hitman could do sitting there tied up and incapacitated, Nate wasn't going to feed him any information about Garrett.

Elsie didn't stop typing and clicking. "He's the one my field operative is with, so he's the one I'm going to search."

Nate didn't want to get all that close to her, not when the soft warmth of her arm in his grasp was still too much a part of him. But he had to lean down and get in close so the hitman didn't overhear. "Garrett isn't shady," he whispered into her ear.

She glared up at him, dark eyes flashing with fury. "How do you know?"

He had to remain in place, and he had to make sure his concern for his brother overrode any sort of physical reaction to being this close to Elsie. "I know my damn brother. I also know his wife. Who cheated on him and up and left out of the blue a year ago. A year…"

The timing of it all came crashing down. It couldn't be… It couldn't…

"What is it?" Elsie asked, some of her anger turning into concern. "Nate. What is it?"

He didn't have to work to whisper this time. His throat was tight and his voice little more than a strangled rasp. "She left right around the same time I told… After all my military contacts didn't believe me about Daria, I started gathering information beyond Daria, right?"

Elsie nodded, leaning even closer so they could continue to have this conversation in a whisper. If his stomach wasn't full of lead, he might have been distracted by how close her lips were to his, but as it was…

Hell.

"I took it all to Garrett. I thought maybe him being in law enforcement and my brother, he'd believe me. Help me. But he didn't. That's when he insisted I join Revival. I thought I'd eventually convince him, but then Savannah left. A few days after that, he found out she'd been having an affair. She just disappeared. I joined Revival, and I left Garrett out of it because he had bigger issues to deal with. How does she connect? Why would she…?" It didn't make *any* sense, but how could the name *and* timing be coincidental?

"What other information do you know about Savannah? Birth date? Where she was born? Anything?" Elsie was typing away, but Nate didn't know much. He'd never really gotten to know Savannah. She'd been very clear she'd thought he was unhinged and wanted nothing to do with him.

So he'd kept his distance as much as she'd kept hers. He hadn't even really blamed her, because everyone thought that about him. But then she'd left and… "I really don't know anything."

If Elsie thought that was weird, she didn't mention it.

"Garrett would know more, obviously, but…"

Elsie waved it away. "I can find records of *their* marriage, and divorce, and go from there." She typed and tapped and her screen zoomed from one window to the next. He didn't understand how she did any of it, or absorbed the information she was skimming. It all went too fast for him.

"Oh. *Oh*," Elsie said breathlessly after only a few minutes.

"Oh. *Oh* what?" Nate leaned closer to the computer, trying to read what Elsie had brought up. "It's a death certificate."

Elsie looked up at him, something warm and caring in her eyes. "She's dead."

"What?" Nate forgot to whisper that demand, but Elsie continued to keep her voice low as she looked back at the screen and read.

"It's from four months ago," Elsie said, pointing to the date on the screen. She used her finger to show him the necessary information as she whispered. "She was admitted to a hospital in Texas. She…" Again Elsie looked up at him. She swallowed. "When did you say she left Blue Valley?"

"About a year ago. Almost exactly." Because it had been summer and he'd finally agreed to join Revival, so he knew to almost the day.

"Um. I don't know how to tell you this." Elsie inhaled

then tapped the section about cause of death. "She died in childbirth. Complications to giving birth to twins."

At this point, Nate's brain was just blank. None of this computed, and he didn't think it ever would. "That doesn't mean..."

"I don't know what it means," Elsie said gently when he didn't finish his sentence. "The twins survived. They were awarded to Savannah's grandparents and... God, there's more, Nate. So much more." She leaned in, and it was like the more she found, the more her nose practically pressed to the screen. "She's related to Courtney."

"How?"

"Cousins. And here's our military connection. Their grandfather, the one who's currently guardian of these babies, is a vice admiral with the Navy."

Nate thought his knees had simply turned to jelly. He remained upright only by gripping the table in front of him, even if it sent a jolt of pain through his injured arm. "I don't understand."

"Neither do I," Elsie said. "But we've got an awful lot to look into."

Chapter Thirteen

Elsie had no luck convincing Nate to sleep—not even reminding him he'd been shot budged him.

She'd kept digging until her eyes had gone blurry and her head was throbbing. Vice Admiral Ray Loren had a squeaky-clean record. She'd gotten nothing interesting from his bank accounts.

The more she didn't find, the more convinced Elsie was that he was the center of everything. But she was reaching the point she simply couldn't get her eyes to focus.

She closed them for a second. She'd just count to one hundred and when she opened them, her eyes would be fine and she could keep digging.

But she heard the snap of her laptop clicking shut and her eyes flew open. She glared at Nate standing there with his hand on her closed laptop. She scowled up at him. "Don't touch my equipment."

"Then be smart. You're not invincible. You're wilting."

Elsie straightened her shoulders. "I know my limits, Nate."

"No, you don't."

"Are you always so arrogant and condescending and bossy?"

"Are you always so determined to take such poor care of yourself? Weren't you just in the hospital or something? Take it easy."

"Oh, yes. Let me *take it easy* right now. Sounds smart."

"Even soldiers have to rest."

"I'm not a soldier, Nate. I think that's obvious. What I can do is find information, sitting here at a computer. It's not a Navy SEAL mission or brain surgery. It's just tapping some keys."

"Just tapping keys." Nate laughed bitterly. "Yeah, that's why my life has been upended. Because you're *just tapping keys*."

Elsie felt unaccountably hurt, like he was blaming her for the twists and turns his life had taken. "I'm just the messenger."

He dragged his hand through his hair. "I know that." He blew out a long breath, because much as he clearly didn't want to admit it, he was as at the end of his rope as she was. "Elsie, take a break from the computer. You said you have a team, right? Get some rest. Just a little."

"And if I get some rest, what will you do?"

He scowled but looked at the watch on his wrist. "We've likely got a few before your friends get here. If you take a break for two hours, I'll take a break for one."

Elsie crossed her arms over her chest and gave him a disparaging look.

"Fine," he muttered. "We'll split the three hours in two, but *only* if you go first."

"Only if you promise to wake me up fair and square under threat of…of… Something bad I'll figure out at a later date."

"Fine. Deal."

She stood and held out her hand so they could shake on it.

There was *something* about the way he looked at her outstretched hand—like he just wasn't so sure about touching her—that made her want to *insist* upon it. She jiggled her hand at him until he scowled.

He closed his much bigger, much rougher, hand over hers and shook. When he tried to release her hand, she held on. She didn't let him pull away. It was a strange impulse.

She just…wanted. And it was probably delirium from lack of sleep. Maybe she was already asleep and this was a dream. That would make a lot of sense, actually. And if it was a dream, she could do anything.

So she stepped close to him. Really close. She looked up at him. He stared down at her warily, but the thing was, he was much bigger and stronger than she was. He could remove his hand from her grip if he wanted to. He could step completely away from her instead of look at her with that expression.

"Nate—"

Then there were three people in the doorway, on top of the hitman bound up in the corner. She hadn't been dreaming, but clearly she'd been delirious. Elsie let out a long breath. "Nate, that's Shay and Gabriel, and I'm assuming you know Connor."

Nate looked at the door, a million emotions crossing his expression before he schooled them into a kind of military stoicism that matched the look on Connor Lindstrom's face.

And Elsie was still standing far too close to Nate, her hand in his. She *knew* she should step away, but her brain wasn't functioning at that level. "You guys are a bit early."

"I guess so," Shay replied. Her voice was cool and even, but Elsie knew her boss well enough to know that didn't mean she wasn't already filing away impressions. Ones that might not look so favorably on Elsie. Still, she stood there.

Nate didn't, though. He pulled his hand free and stepped back from Elsie.

"Let's load up our friend here," Shay said, nodding at the hitman whose furious expression hadn't changed the whole time he'd been sitting there. "Gabriel?"

Gabriel moved into the cabin and to the hitman. Lee Braun didn't struggle as Gabe dragged him outside. Elsie figured he knew he didn't have any hope against *four* ex-soldiers and/or highly trained operatives.

"Why don't you and I step outside while Connor and Nate get reacquainted?" Shay said, raising an eyebrow at Elsie. She made it sound like a question, but Elsie knew it was most certainly not an invitation. It was an order.

She didn't look back at Nate or make eye contact

with Connor. She just forced herself to smile and follow Shay outside.

There was the faintest hint of dawn in the east, the storm having passed over and leaving the world shiny and new. Gabriel was in a very tactical-looking boat, loading the hitman up and then motoring into the dark.

Shay was quiet and still as the boat slowly disappeared. The sound of the water lapping against the shore mixed with the chill of the early morning should have given Elsie some space to find her bearings, but her exhaustion was making her emotional for absolutely no reason.

Shay said nothing. Elsie had to break the silence or burst into inexplicable tears. "You guys got here fast," she said cheerily. "Aren't bosses supposed to stay behind and delegate?"

Shay laughed. "Yeah, supposed to. But this is getting big, and Holden's back at his farm with his wife. *Wife.* Sabrina's out of commission for a while. I even tried to convince Reece to come back, but that was a no go."

"You have other operatives."

"I know. Gabriel and Mallory work well together, and they're definitely in the running for taking lead roles. But we're talking military higher-ups. I thought we needed all hands on deck."

"You miss the field," Elsie said, feeling for her boss. Shay was an excellent head of North Star, but the leader so often had to sit back and pull strings and coordinate. Not *do*. Shay wasn't the kind of woman who liked to sit around pushing papers.

Shay shrugged. "I've been in the field plenty this year."

"Yeah, because you miss it."

"Maybe I do." Shay looked at Elsie. "And you don't want to be in it, so you can go back to headquarters, Els. We'll take it from here. I don't want you going with Gabe and the hitman, so we'll have you—"

"What?" Her stomach sank like a rock. Go back? *Leave?* "Wait. I can't leave."

"You did what we needed you to do. We made contact with Nate without anyone being suspicious. You've uncovered deeper connections. Mallory can—"

"You can't send me back to headquarters."

Shay's eyebrows rose. "I can't?"

Elsie swallowed. So many emotions battered around inside her, and she *was* exhausted, so she didn't know how to catalog or deal with them all. "My family could be in the crosshairs. I should be here. On the ground. With you guys."

"You don't trust us to keep your family safe?" Shay asked, her voice carefully devoid of any emotion.

Elsie knew her boss well enough to read the surprise. And the hurt. "You know that's not it, Shay," Elsie said.

Shay eyed her. "What's really going on, Els?"

"I just…know these people. Not just my family, but I grew up with them. Garrett Averly tried to help my sisters and me when almost no one in this town ever did. Nate is…"

Shay's eyebrows rose farther and Elsie knew she couldn't afford to blush, but the heat was creeping into her cheeks anyway.

"I'm no operative, but I need to see this through. Don't send me back, Shay. Please."

NATE DIDN'T KNOW how to talk to Connor. All of a sudden, this friend of his, who Nate was responsible for dragging into this mess—from the very beginning— was here. Standing in the cabin.

"We should probably search the island," Connor said. "Make sure no one else is here. It'd be a good base, I'd think."

"I'd think," Nate echoed. The hitman was gone. Elsie was outside. And he was standing in his brother's fishing cabin in the middle of Montana. But it was like he was back in the Middle East. Sand in his mouth and Connor standing there—tall and honorable—wondering what Nate was dragging him into.

Yet this time, Connor was in some…group. They weren't on the same team, even if they were hoping for the same end result. "You're just a part of this group now?" Nate asked, not knowing how else to break the oppressive silence between them.

"Yeah," Connor said. Effusive as always.

"I thought you liked search and rescue?"

"I love it. But this is similar. Well, except for the fact I had to leave my dog back at headquarters."

"Why would you leave something you love for something 'similar'?"

Connor shrugged. "Sabrina's there."

Nate didn't wince exactly. "I guess that's a weird topic of conversation." Nate's ex. Connor's current. Yeah, that was weird.

"I guess."

Brina in a hospital somewhere. "How's she doing?"

"Okay." A ghost of a smile flitted with Connor's mouth. "Mouthy and irritable, so she's getting better."

Nate shoved his hands in his pockets.

Connor took a deep breath and slowly let it out. It was only when he spoke, Nate finally understood what all this awkwardness was really about.

"You were right. All this time."

"So it appears," Nate agreed. Connor's guilt didn't sit right, though. "I didn't always believe myself, so don't take it so hard."

"But you were right."

"And Elsie's theory is that someone or *someones* were working to discredit every accusation I made. It's hard to trust a guy who's been blown to hell when none of the evidence supports his theories."

"Except the evidence you supplied."

"I wasn't a trustworthy source. I didn't always see that at the time, but I get it now. And I don't have any hard feelings. You shouldn't, either."

Connor studied him in that silence Connor had always done so well. Eventually he smiled. Imperceptibly.

"So, what now?" Nate asked.

Connor shook his head. "I guess we sort through this mess and figure out who tried to ruin our lives."

"And stop them."

Connor nodded. "I'm not sure we could have done that on our own, Nate, but I think we can do it with North Star."

"Then let's get to work." Before Nate could move,

Shay and Elsie reentered the cabin. Their expressions were inscrutable. The tall, built blonde and the slim, brilliant brunette.

"Okay, let's get up to speed about what happens next," the blonde said. Shay. The boss. There was no doubt that everyone would do as she said.

"Gabriel is taking the hitman to our military contacts—good guys, I promise. He'll be interrogated there, and we'll get all the pertinent information. One of Elsie's people found a connection to Ross Industries. It's very slight, but considering the hitman was still after Nate even after North Star took down Daria, we're looking beyond Daria. Elsie said you've got evidence, Nate."

"Some. I gave her everything I had. She's got far more skills than me."

"She's got far more skills than everyone," Shay said proudly. "So, she'll keep gathering information. You can't go back to Revival," she said firmly. "There's no way to hide the fact the hitman came for you, that Don waited for you, and they've been arrested. Anyone after you, or who thinks you're a threat, knows you're involved in something fighting that now. This is a good place that we can easily defend. We'll have men on the ground around the island and you'll stay put here."

"How does this connect to the Lorens?" Nate asked.

"That, we don't know yet," Elsie said, clearly trying to hide a yawn. She opened her laptop and Nate thought briefly of when he'd closed it. When she'd held his hand. When…

Not the time for that. Shay was continuing on, reminding him of many a commanding officer he'd had in the Navy.

"No one knows Elsie's connected. So, I'm going to get her back to her sister's and hopefully no one suspects she was gone tonight. She'll communicate with us from there."

Nate glanced at Elsie, but she was frowning at her laptop. She needed some rest. She needed…probably quiet to focus on her task. Them separating was for the best. For both of them.

So, why did it feel like a loss?

"Mallory should be back from Blue Valley any minute, and Gabriel will return by afternoon. I'm staying on, so we'll have four operatives on the island."

Nate began to shake his head. It didn't seem like anyone was going to argue with Shay, but she was missing an important piece of all this. "Someone needs to be on Elsie."

"They don't know I'm connected," Elsie said with a frown.

"That we know of. If Courtney Prokop's brother is involved, he knows there's rumors about Elsie and me."

"Rumors?" Shay said, looking at Elsie, eyebrows raised.

Elsie blushed, but Nate couldn't care about that. "If someone's been watching—and someone had to be to know I tried to send Connor evidence—they could have easily been watching me. Who knows who Don communicated with before Mallory went out there and he tried to ambush her? We don't know who's out there, who's watching, or for how long. How can you send her to Revival without someone watching out for her?"

Everyone in the room looked at him like he had grown a third head. He was used to that. God, he was so much more used to that than people believing him and making plans around the things he'd thought for years.

Shay's expression changed, imperceptibly, bit by bit. "He's right," she finally said, clearly a little shocked by the fact. "We don't fully know if Elsie's been compromised." She looked back at Elsie, her expression grim. "I guess you're going to have to stay here."

Chapter Fourteen

Relief coursed through Elsie, even if it shouldn't. How was she going to explain this to her sisters? That she'd stayed with them a few days then up and disappeared—leaving a majority of her equipment behind.

But no matter how guilty she felt over that, she got to *stay*. She got to continue to be part of this. If they'd shipped her back to Revival, she'd always be a step behind, doling out information as she found it, not as it happened in front of her. It was for the best that she stay here.

For the best.

And had absolutely everything to do with wanting to be close to Nate, to continue to work with him on this. Together. She understood that, even as she told herself it was stupid and way beyond the point. She couldn't help it. They'd become…a team in these short few days.

She needed to see this through *with* him.

Mallory entered the small cabin, so that it was now chock-full of people with not a lot of space to breathe. But no one acted like that was weird or uncomfortable as Mallory explained she'd gotten Don situated with

Garrett and some new security and North Star communications.

But then Mallory's gaze turned to Elsie with some apology in her expression. "Uh, Els. Your sister was in the police station when I left."

Since those words didn't make sense together, Elsie could only manage one word. "What?"

"Yelling at Garrett. Demanding to know what Nate had done with you."

"Oh. Dear," Elsie managed. She didn't look at Nate. She didn't look at anything except her computer.

"Garrett was handling it okay, but I'm pretty sure anyone in a ten-mile radius is going to know Els and Nate are connected, and if more people are out there looking at Nate..."

"Yeah, we know," Shay said on a sigh. "We've already decided to keep Elsie here. But someone is going to have to shut the sister up."

"I'll call her," Elsie said, dread filling her as she forced herself to sound firm and in control. "I'll get her to stop looking for me and making demands. But if the wrong person *did* hear her... Shay, you have to make sure no one hurts Revival."

"Like we aren't spread thin enough. I'll call in—"

"Shay. I need *you* to make sure no one hurts Revival. Not part-timers or friends you call in for a favor. This is my *family*, who don't even connect to what's happening. I need someone I trust. Someone I know will—"

"What about Granger?"

Elsie stopped on a dime. Granger Macmillan had been the first leader of North Star. When he'd been injured, Shay had taken over. Granger had gone off to some mysterious ranch deep in the mountains and, for a while, only Shay had known where he was. It was just in the past few months that Shay had been getting him to come back and help with missions—though he wouldn't return to the group officially no matter how they tried to convince him.

Still, Elsie trusted Granger just as much as Shay and the rest of the full-time North Star team. He'd hired her. Believed in her. He would protect her family, she was sure of it. "All right."

"I'll give him a call. You call your sister and make damn sure she shuts up about everything. And don't go telling her…"

"I know," Elsie said. She managed a paltry smile.

North Star was, and stayed, a secret for a wide variety of reasons. Elsie might not always have a clear idea of what those were, but she was the one who often wiped a person's history for them. Then put it back when they decided to rejoin civilian life. She could make things disappear and create fictions that everyone in the world would take as fact. She had *no* idea how she was going to convince her sister to stand down. She couldn't even give Shay an I-told-you-so about her not belonging in the field, because she very much wanted to stay in *this* particular field for reasons that were entirely inappropriate.

"Can I go outside to do this in private?"

Shay shook her head. "We'll go out. Plan where we're going to be." She nodded her head at the door and the team, including Nate, followed her outside. Nate did give Elsie one look over his shoulder, but she couldn't really read anything in it.

Right now, she had bigger fish to fry. She closed her eyes and gave a quick prayer for some kind of genius lie to pop into her head, and then dialed Rose's cell.

"So help me God, Elsie Marie Rogers, I am so furious with you, but if you're hurt or need help, tell me when and where and—"

"Sissy, I'm fine. What are you doing up so early?"

"I have two kids and a husband who works on a ranch—and don't think you're going to get around this by wondering why I'm up so early. Where are you? What's happened? If Nate Averly put his hands on you—"

"He hasn't. It isn't like that, Rose." She blew out a breath and rolled her eyes at herself. She should have gone along with it. Said she was in love with him or something ridiculous. Swept off and away by a dashing cowboy.

Besides, she kind of wished Nate Averly had put his hands on her. But that was beside the point.

"Explain. Now," Rose demanded.

"Are you still at the police station?"

"Damn right I'm at the police station. How do you know that? Where are you, Elsie? Why would you scare me like this?"

Me. Well, that was something. "So you haven't told anyone else?"

"I wasn't going to worry Delia until I had to. Jack knows, obviously. But he's home with the kids and…

Why am I explaining myself to you? Explain to me what is going on."

Elsie wished she could tell her sister the whole unvarnished truth, but maybe… Maybe she could give her enough. Maybe it would be enough.

"I can't tell you everything. I wish I could, but it's not… This is all part of my job. I promise you, I'm safe and sound. But sometimes I have to move fast. I thought I'd be back by morning and you wouldn't have to worry, but now I have to stay away for a bit."

"Stay away? With Nate Averly. I do not think so."

"My job helps people, sissy. *I* help people. Right now, I'm helping Nate. He's in trouble, and my team and I are going to get him out of it."

There was a long pause on Rose's end and Elsie felt like holding her breath. Would her sister buy any of this?

"So, you work for people who use your computer genius to help people?"

"Yes, and that's all I can tell you. For your own safety, okay?"

"Safety. Are you in danger? You didn't look right. Were you hurt? Is this—?"

"Rose. Listen to me. I got this job because I know computers and information. I've helped save people for three years. Innocent people. Good people. In those three years, I've only been in real, serious danger twice, and I always came out the other side, because there are people who know what they're doing protecting me. But I found myself here, and I promise you I am not just good—I need this. Now, I need you not to worry. I need you to…"

"I will damn well worry," Rose said.

"Okay, then I need you to trust me. To believe me. I know what I'm doing. I'm good at what I'm doing. It's why I don't come home much. I wouldn't have come home this time, but the job was Nate. So, it made sense."

"None of this makes any sense. Are you a spy or something?"

"Not…exactly."

Rose laughed, though it was more baffled than amused. "Elsie…"

"I know it's a lot to swallow, but I wouldn't lie to you like this. You know that, right? I wouldn't make up this far-fetched thing. We've been through too much, come too far. Please. Believe me."

Rose was quiet for long enough that Elsie knew she was seriously thinking about what Elsie had said. "I just need to know you're okay."

"I'm okay. I'm better than okay. This job…" Elsie's throat got tight. "It saved me. It showed me who I could be. I can't do my job if you're in Blue Valley yelling at Garrett. I need you to go home and…take care of your babies and your husband. I promise you, once this mission is over…I'll come home and spend some time. For real. No job. You can see just how good I am."

"Mission. Hell, Elsie. I…" She blew out a long breath.

Elsie didn't know what else to say to convince Rose. To make her understand.

When Rose spoke, it was with a fierceness that had always been with her. Because Rose was fierce and strong and, honestly, Elsie wasn't sure how she was the one at home with babies and Elsie was the one fighting roving gangs and military corruption with an elite, secret group.

But here they were.

"If this is all on the up-and-up, and you're really some secret spy or whatever, then I'm proud of you. Amazed by you. But if you get yourself hurt, I'm going to kill you and everyone involved myself."

Elsie managed a laugh as she tried to fight the wave of emotion and tears. "Deal," she croaked. She cleared her throat. "I have to go."

"Please…keep in touch as much as possible."

"I will. And I'll be home soon."

"Good. Take care of yourself, Els."

"I will. Bye." Elsie clicked the end button. She wouldn't cry. There were a bunch of tough operatives and military men out there who'd probably never cried a day in their lives. She had to be strong. Even if Rose's trust and belief and *pride* meant everything to her. Filled up an empty space she hadn't known she still had.

"Oh, screw it," she rasped into the silence of the cabin. She gave in and let herself cry.

WHILE ELSIE TALKED to her sister, Shay laid out the island, and where she wanted pairs stationed. She put Connor and Mallory together on the east side, and said she'd be on the west with Gabriel when he returned. It was a small enough island. That should keep the cabin protected.

"What about me?" Nate asked once she'd made the assignments clear.

Shay eyed him carefully. "You're on Elsie duty.

Whatever info you've got that she needs, supply it. You'll also be the contact to your brother." She nodded to his bandaged arm. "That doesn't look too bad, but it's a weakness we can't afford out here."

Nate didn't know what to say to that. He should be annoyed by the assignment. Annoyed by her calling a little gunshot wound a weakness.

But he wasn't.

"While Elsie and her team at headquarters keep digging, we watch and wait for more hitmen or what have you. If we get anything on the original hitman, the info will be sent around. If we need to meet, we'll do it at the cabin. Consider it our epicenter for the time being."

There were nods and murmurs of assent.

"Right now, we're in a waiting phase until we've got information to move forward on. Any threats we run into, we just want to neutralize and ideally use to further our mission."

"What *is* our mission?"

Shay looked at Nate, and he couldn't figure out what she saw, what she thought. But she spoke with a clarity and surety that helped center him.

"To take down the group using the military to arm and fund their unlawful purposes, to bring all perpetrators to justice, and to keep you, your brother and all members of my team safe in the process. Does that work for you?"

"Yeah, it does."

"Good." She nodded to Connor and Mallory. "Let's get situated." They started to move away, but Connor stood where he was, studying Nate.

Per usual, he said nothing for the longest time. When he finally spoke, he held out his hand. "See you on the other side."

Other side. Nate had sort of stopped believing in another side. An end to this. A world where he got to—not just be believed, but vindicated.

He shook Connor's hand and then watched his friend melt into the trees, feeling a bit like there was quicksand under his feet.

The other side.

What life was he going to have on the other side?

Nate stared at the cabin door. He didn't let his mind go there. One step at a time. Elsie was the current step.

God help him.

He walked into the cabin then stopped short.

Elsie sat on her tiny chair, but she was sniffling. Her cheeks were tearstained, the tip of her nose red. She wiped at her face in an attempt to clean herself up, but she didn't exactly hide the fact she'd been crying.

"Everything okay?" Nate asked warily.

She nodded. "Got my sister to stand down." She stood and started fussing in the kitchenette. "Took some doing." She flitted from one thing to the next—sink, counter, table—without settling anywhere or completing any task. "But she said…she said she was proud of me." Her voice cracked and, though her back was to him, he had the impression she was crying again.

"That's…bad?"

"No. It's wonderful," she squeaked. "And awful."

"I really don't follow."

She kept her back to him, but shook her head. Then

her shoulders began to shake, though she made no sound.

Hell.

He had half a thought to leave the cabin. To let her have her inexplicable emotional moment while he went…far away. But that would be cowardly. She'd had a long few days. What she really needed was some rest.

He crossed the small room with the thought he'd tell her that. Maybe pull her along to the couch so she'd rest. Yeah, that's what he'd do. Gently, he placed his hand on her shoulder and turned her to face him.

But instead of moving with his hand, or away from his grasp, she stepped right into him. Burying her face in his chest.

Nate held himself perfectly still. What…was he supposed to *do*? He was not used to emotional breakdowns. He'd never seen his mother cry. He was pretty sure she'd jump off a cliff first. He'd grown up and worked mostly around men. Never had much of a long-term relationship, aside from Brina—and if his mother was rock-solid, Brina was granite.

But he couldn't remain immobile while Elsie cried into his shirt. He slowly and carefully wrapped his arms around her and held her there. Crying against his chest. She softened into him, like it was exactly the right move.

Like this was exactly right.

"I just hate that they're worried about me," she said, her voice muffled. "That they're somehow dragged into this. And it isn't just them. Poor Garrett. He doesn't even know his full connection yet, and I'm sorry."

"You're sorry?"

"My group."

He held her a little tighter. "My digging. Don't blame yourself for any of this. You said it yourself. You're just the messenger."

"I've never had to be the messenger to people I care about before."

People I care about. She meant her sisters. Surely not him.

Dangerous ground.

"Come on." He led her over to the couch and nudged her into a sitting position, but she just looked up at him like he could…fix this. He hadn't fixed a damn thing in so long, it was like being in a tractor beam. He had to sit next to her, to put his arm around her and let her curl up against him.

They sat on the couch together like it was normal. Like he comforted her all the time and it just felt right to sit here cozied up together. He had never wished for a future that didn't simply involve everyone who thought he was crazy realizing he wasn't. He'd never gone any further than that.

Until now.

"You're going to have to call Garrett," Elsie said after a while. She yawned as she said it and he wondered if he held still enough, if she'd finally doze off. She'd stopped crying, but he knew she was hardly over the emotional upheaval.

"Do we have to tell Garrett about Savannah?" Nate asked. "Couldn't we just… It's bad enough she cheated and left, now he's got to know he was some weird pawn in we don't even know what."

"I need more info on her, and he might have it. I think I'd rather know I was a pawn and cheated on and left than think it was *real* and I was cheated on and left."

"You do not know my brother." But Elsie was right. It wasn't about what Garrett would rather know. It was what he needed to know. "I'll want to tell him in person. Over the phone…it isn't right. It needs to be in person."

"Did he love her?"

Nate didn't shift, but only because Elsie was leaning against him. Love didn't seem like the best topic of conversation. But how could he ignore it? "I assume so. Garrett isn't the kind of guy who'd get married without taking that commitment really seriously." Commitment. Marriage. How were they talking about this?

Elsie lifted her head from his shoulder, which felt like a loss. But then she looked into his eyes and he didn't know what to do but meet that warm gaze. Her hand was on his shoulder and they were still hip to hip.

"Maybe she loved him, too," Elsie said hopefully. "Maybe that's why she ran away?"

"While she was pregnant with twins?"

Elsie wilted a little, but she didn't give up. "Maybe she was trying to save Garrett from something."

"I could maybe believe that if she wasn't related to Courtney. You might not believe me, but that woman is a snake."

"A person can't be judged by their family members."

"Maybe not," Nate agreed, knowing she was thinking about herself and her parents. "But it's a lot of co-incidences to believe in love."

That word seemed to echo between them, and Nate really, *really* didn't know what to do with that. He'd never considered himself bad or awkward at interactions with the opposite sex, but the Nate who'd come back from war, injured and dishonorably discharged, and certain he'd been about to uncover something terrible…was not the same Nate Averly who'd left.

Elsie leaned forward, eyes on his. There was no subterfuge, certainly no mistaking that look. It and she should have been easy to resist. There was nothing particularly seductive about the move. She looked a mess from crying and he should…

Her lips touched his. Soft, but not tentative. Just gentle. Like *he* was fragile. Or they were. Together.

That gentleness made the kiss impossible to break. He knew—God, he knew—this was wrong, but no amount of knowing changed what he felt. What he did as he smoothed his hand over her hair, changed the angle of the kiss.

Her hands on his face felt like a new lease on life. Erasing the past few years and building something new and possible right here in this moment.

Which you know isn't possible. Thankfully, that thought managed to penetrate. He eased away from her mouth. He had to clear his throat to talk. "Elsie."

She opened her eyes on a sigh. "I know. You're not… It's okay. You're not into me. I get it."

"Not… What?" He got to his feet and raked his hands

through his hair. What was his life? "I kissed you back, Elsie. It's not a question of being into you."

She blinked then smiled. That was bad. Very bad. He had to put a stop to that self-satisfied smile or he might forget there were three or four other people on this island waiting around for a threat against *him*. *He* was in danger and…

He had to nip this in the bud. Immediately. No matter how that kiss had rearranged things inside him. "It's a stressful situation and I'm just not sure you're seeing things clearly."

She shook her head. "No. Don't ruin it. I kissed you. You kissed me back. It was nice. Let's leave it at that."

Wait. "Nice?"

"Don't get all bent out of shape. It *was* nice." She smiled up at him innocently.

"I see what you're doing. You're not going to goad me into this."

She quirked an eyebrow at him like that's exactly what she was going to do.

Maybe she was.

Chapter Fifteen

Elsie felt like a live wire. And something more. A blooming flower. A cart of dynamite with the fuse lit. She felt all these *amazing* things she'd never felt. Not once.

It was all ridiculous and she didn't care. The voice of reason telling her she was exhausted and delirious had died when his lips had touched hers. She would have backed away after the kiss if Nate had said he wasn't into her. Let it go.

But he *was* interested. Just too…noble or something.

She stood and crossed to him. He didn't retreat, which was probably as much ingrained habit as anything else. Nate wasn't a man who backed down from a challenge.

So, she'd challenge him.

She knew the timing was terrible, but her whole life was full of terrible timing. If there was one thing she'd learned, it was that you had to take whatever came, whenever it came.

She wanted to take Nate.

"Your friends are out there," he said, sounding vaguely strangled as she slid her hands up his chest.

"My coworkers," Elsie agreed, studying him as she linked her fingers behind his neck. There was something adorable at how stiff and uncomfortable he was. Because he was *not* unmoved. That much was clear. "Outside this cabin. With us inside. Alone."

"I should tell Garrett," he said somewhat desperately. "About everything. With his ex-wife."

"Now you want to tell Garrett?"

"Yeah, I should. I'll call him."

"You didn't want to do it over the phone," she reminded him.

"Oh. Right." He swallowed. "Elsie."

She looked up at him, sure she would come up with something pithy and challenging to say, but his gaze was so dark, so…intent. "What?"

He sucked in a breath then seemed to find some iron will. Gently, he pulled her hands from around his neck and nudged her back a step. Before she could do anything to retaliate, he took her face in his hands. His expression was so serious, she actually paused. It wasn't a game, she knew that. But she also knew that for some people sex could be casual. Easy. Something to move on from.

Eventually.

But he didn't look any of those things. He held her face and looked deep into her eyes. "I don't want you to misunderstand me. It's not that I don't *want* to, but it shouldn't be like this."

"Be like what?"

"In the middle of all this. In my brother's tiny fishing cabin. Not some fumbling impulse."

"I'm sorry...you'd rather plan it out?"

His grip on her face tightened and he leaned forward, so serious. So...Nate. "I'd rather it *mean* something."

Her heart fluttered, like a fragile butterfly. Something she'd been very careful to avoid her entire adult life. Anything too fragile, including herself and her own feelings. She'd needed armor and North Star had given it to her and now Nate was...

All her bravado and certainty fled. *This* wasn't what she was looking for. *This* was dangerous ground. Because this was real, and he was talking about...the kinds of things she'd always avoided without fully realizing that's what she was doing.

Now she wanted to lean into all that she'd avoided, even knowing it was dangerous. Even as her mind yelled warnings at her, her heart reminded her that he'd held her when she'd cried, and they understood each other in this strange, complicated way. He knew who she was and he didn't *treat* her differently because of what she'd endured.

She felt completely immobilized by all of this. Want and need and a genuine care she hadn't counted on. She didn't care for it, but it was inside of her. Blooming against her will.

Still, Nate's hands were on her face. Still, he looked at her intently. "It's not the time. And I won't be the same guy on the other side of this."

She reached up and covered his hands with hers. Because she knew that excuse. She knew that belief. It had been a core part of how she'd struggled once she'd gotten away from her father and Blue Valley. "Yes, you will."

"You don't understand." He tried to pull his hands away, and though he got them off her face, she gripped them before he could withdraw completely.

"No, I do. When you go through a trauma, you think eventually you'll move past it, heal from it and be some new, shiny thing. But you won't. You're still you. You can heal, but you don't become a new person."

He pressed her hand against his heart. He didn't say anything. Just looked at her like she'd sliced him in two.

This was the part she couldn't walk away from. How *much* she understood. No matter how scared, how worried, that this little glow was breakable and could ruin everything, it was the understanding that kept her rooted to the spot. Staring at him. Waiting for…

And then it was too late, whatever this was. Mallory was in the doorway. If she'd heard anything, she didn't let it show. "We've got company."

NATE FINALLY MANAGED to get himself out of Elsie's grasp. Not because she'd been stronger than him, but because all that emotion and connection was finally broken by a third party.

And he could remember who he was, not what he wanted to be.

Even if the next few pieces of this proved he was right all along, it didn't…

Elsie had said it herself. It didn't change who he was. A man who'd spent the past two years of his life mired in the past. He didn't have a job. The future was unclear—because in the past he'd only been working toward proving he wasn't insane.

Elsie had this job she loved. She was a *genius* putting her skills to work to help people. Nate had only ever been after helping himself.

"It's Courtney Prokop. Alone. Unarmed," Mallory stated grimly.

"That doesn't make any sense," Elsie said, frowning.

"No, it doesn't," Mallory agreed. She looked at Nate. "But we thought you could be out there to help greet her while we figure out what she thinks she's doing."

Nate nodded. "You'll stay put with Elsie?"

"Yeah."

"I'm not some weakling who needs protecting," Elsie said, frowning at both of them.

"No, but it's hard to point a gun when you're eyeballs-deep in the computer screen like you usually are," Mallory said, giving a much better explanation than Nate would have. She was no weakling, but that didn't mean she had to turn down protection.

Elsie huffed out a breath. "Fine. Babysit me," she muttered. "I'm going to find out what Courtney Prokop is up to."

Mallory nodded at the door, a clear sign Nate was supposed to go. He found he didn't want to. He didn't want to face Courtney. He didn't want to deal with all the inexplicable happenings around him.

He wanted to stay right here with Elsie.

And that wasn't an option. He stepped outside. Morning had dawned, pearly and pretty. Courtney's boat was nearing the dock. A small canoe she was paddling. Odd. This whole thing was bizarre.

Nate stood at the dock and scanned his surroundings without moving a muscle. Though he couldn't see anything except a little glint of reflection, he could tell someone was positioned right behind the cabin, eyes on him and Courtney. Nate believed it was Shay since it seemed there was only one person. He presumed she was purposefully letting him see that she was there.

But Courtney likely wouldn't know, unless she was trained to look for some kind of small hint that something was amiss.

Who knew? Maybe she was.

Still, Nate didn't let his gaze linger on the person behind the cabin. He focused on Courtney as she docked and then tied up her canoe. She stepped onto the dock.

"Oh, Nate. I'm *so* sorry." She came right up to him and flung her arms around him like they were old friends. Or more than.

Nate stood stock-still. He didn't understand anything that was going on, but felt his only course of action was to let it unfold. Much as he'd like to push her off and demand what the hell was going on.

"What are you doing here?"

She looked up at him from underneath her lashes. She looked distraught, but Nate found himself utterly unmoved. He'd seen her emotionally manipulate a few too many people—her brother, her supposed husband, some of the other men at Revival—to believe that she couldn't just put on a mask whenever she wanted.

"I just couldn't live with it any longer."

"Live with what?"

"The truth." She sucked in a breath. "I have a bag in the boat. You're not going to hurt me if I grab it, are you?"

"You're not going to hurt me if I let you, are you?"

She smiled and patted his chest, letting her hand linger. "I promise, Nate. I'm here to help you. We've been pawns in an awful thing, and I just couldn't live with myself if I didn't tell you."

Nate didn't let his distrust or his unease show. She pulled a messenger-type bag out of the canoe and then slung it over her shoulder. "Can we go into the cabin?" she said, pointing at it in the distance.

Nate looked at the cabin. No doubt Mallory was watching, same as Shay. Maybe even Elsie. He looked back at Courtney and the way she was gripping the bag.

"I'm going to have to look through the bag first."

She sighed and held it out to him. "I totally understand. You've been through so much. You have every right to be paranoid."

He took the bag, trying to keep his movements practical and devoid of emotion even though he wanted to jerk it out of her grasp. "Paranoid isn't the word I'd use." He looked through every pocket, but the only thing inside was a laptop and a cord. The computer looked legit. Elsie would know if it hid explosives or could trigger something.

But he was hardly going to take this woman into the cabin with Elsie.

He handed the bag back to her. "Why don't you tell me what you've got to tell me here?"

"I'm afraid it's something I have to *show* you. I need an outlet of some kind. What do you think I'm going to do? Kill you?"

Nate shrugged.

Courtney rolled her eyes. "Nate. Honestly. You were a Navy SEAL. You can take me." She smiled up at him. "I promise."

Nate didn't know what else to do but agree. He walked toward the cabin, keeping his pace slow. Hopefully, he was giving Mallory and Elsie enough time to hide if they needed to.

He didn't trust Courtney for a second, so it was probably best if she didn't know he now had an entire group helping him out.

Unless she already *did* know. It was hard to say what anyone did or didn't know. But it was worth a few minutes, he supposed, to figure out what she was trying to pull over on him.

Nate opened the door and stepped inside, once again standing still as he scanned the area around him. No sign of Elsie or Mallory, or even Elsie's things. Good.

Courtney brushed past him, unnecessarily, on her way in. Nate really couldn't figure out her angle, so he just kept his mouth shut.

"Let's see." She wandered the interior of the cabin and then settled herself at the table Elsie had been situated at not that long ago. It made Nate frown even though he was trying to maintain an unemotional expression.

He'd much rather be staring at Elsie eating her granola bars and ruining her eyes than Courtney plugging in her laptop and then tapping some keys.

Nate forced himself to move over to her. Best to know what she was doing just in case that computer *was* a threat.

She brought up some kind of video player. "I know this is going to upset you, but I knew you deserved the truth."

Garrett appeared on the screen. With his ex-wife. Nate recognized the room as the kitchen in their house, a cozy Craftsman just off Main Street where Garrett could walk to the police station and Savannah could walk to her job as a cashier at the hardware store.

"You have to convince him to enroll at Revival," Savannah was saying.

"For his own safety?" Garrett asked. He was sitting at the kitchen table and Savannah put a mug of coffee in front of him. In the corner of the screen, Nate could see Barney snoring away on the floor.

"Of course," Savannah said but then smiled. "And 'for his own safety' will become for our own gain."

Nate frowned. That didn't make any sense.

"What if he suspects something?" Garrett asked, sounding less worried and more…practical about the whole thing. Very Garrett.

"He suspects everything. Isn't that the point?" Savannah stood behind Garrett and wrapped her arms around his neck. "And if he's at Revival, your parents are going to take him off their will."

Garrett smiled and patted his wife's hand. "That is the plan. Mom and Dad bought the box of fake information hook, line and sinker. They're convinced he's crazy."

"Well, he is. So, we're doing him a favor."

Garrett pulled Savannah onto his lap, nuzzled her neck. "We're doing ourselves a bigger one, and that's what really matters."

Nate didn't move. It was like being turned to ash in a matter of seconds. His brother. Working with his ex-wife. To discredit him. To make him seem so unhinged their parents would make Garrett sole inheritor.

It didn't make sense. Mom and Dad's property was small, and they were only in their late fifties and in excellent health. Why would Garrett be concerned about their estate? Garrett had never been concerned about money.

But Savannah had, and Garrett had loved Savannah. Would he have done…anything for her?

"I'm sorry, Nate," Courtney said.

Nate barely registered the words. He was still looking at the computer screen, the image now frozen. Garrett and Savannah in what he knew to be their kitchen. Barney was there. It was just…an actual scene out of their life from a year ago.

Courtney rose and put her hand on his shoulder. She stood between him and the screen so that he had to look at her instead of it.

"We're just innocent victims in this, Nate," she said sadly.

He stared at Courtney. He'd been taken in there for a while. Watched his brother say horrible things and believed them. For a few minutes, his world had crashed around him.

But listening to Courtney say *innocent victims* like she was somehow part of this—when what would it matter to her if he'd been discredited? Something was a fraud here.

And he didn't think it was his brother.

"How are you a victim?"

"Someone is blackmailing me. They said I had to show you this, even though I knew it would wreck you."

"Someone?"

"I don't know who. I was just given instructions to show you this. I'm not supposed to tell you it's blackmail, but my heart's just breaking for you, Nate. I'm so sorry and—"

"What are they blackmailing you with?"

Courtney blinked then looked at the floor. She was a damn good actress…if she was acting.

She *had* to be. Garrett didn't care about estates. Savannah had left him. This had to be fraudulent. Somehow. Some way.

"Well…Don and I aren't really married."

That was true. Elsie had found out that was true. Could Courtney actually be…telling the truth? Could this awful thing be real?

"Why don't you come back to Blue Valley with me, Nate? I'd hate for you to be out here alone. Feeling so hopeless, like it might not be worth it to go on," Courtney said, leaning her head against his shoulder.

Much like Elsie had. But Elsie had belonged there. Elsie told the truth.

He didn't know what this woman was doing, but it wasn't anything to do with the truth. It couldn't be. He knew better than anyone that when things didn't add up, no matter how real they looked to other people, you kept digging until the math worked.

"Are you trying to get me to commit suicide, Courtney?"

She pulled back, eyes wide, her hand fluttering to her chest. "Nate. How can you say such a thing? I'm going to insist you come back with me. You have a therapist at Revival, don't you?"

"You should go now, Courtney," he said, not bothering to hide the ice in his tone. "You can leave the laptop."

"I can't do that." She moved to it and packed it away again. "I have to give it to my blackmailers."

"At least give me a copy of the video."

Courtney shook her head. "It would only depress you farther, Nate. The truth was enough. Don't go doing something drastic—"

"You can go now." Maybe Elsie could dig up a copy through her computer hacking or something. Or maybe she'd seen something or… It didn't matter. He needed Courtney out of his orbit.

"Don't be angry," she said, her eyes sad and her voice pleading.

Nate remained unmoved. "Goodbye, Courtney."

She lifted onto her toes and pressed a kiss to his cheek, for far longer than was necessary. Her hands trailed down his chest and pulled away just at his waistband. "You can always call me, Nate. I promise, you can trust me."

He pointed to the door and she left, bag on her shoulder, with just the hint of a frown.

Nate scowled after her.

He'd trust Satan himself first.

Chapter Sixteen

Elsie wondered if Nate had any idea she'd set up a camera and microphone that enabled her and Mallory to watch everything that happened from where they hunched in the woods.

She watched Courtney brush past Nate as she sauntered into the cabin and wanted to do a bunch of violent things she'd promised herself she'd never want to engage in. But having a violent thought in anger and acting on it were two different things, as her therapist had always told her.

Nate seemed unaffected. He played it well—neither acted too suspicious of her nor too comfortable with her as she pulled out a laptop.

"This is weird," Mallory muttered, though her gaze didn't stay on the screen but instead kept scanning their surroundings as if she half expected someone to jump out and surprise them all.

Elsie couldn't look away from the screen. She could make out what Courtney was showing Nate. It was a video. It looked like Garrett and some woman in a kitchen. The voices from the video were quiet but clear enough to make out.

Elsie's heart sank to her toes. She felt *sick* over this. Garrett was saying awful things. Hadn't she considered that it was an option? That he was somehow in on it. The ex-wife was dead, even if the babies weren't and...

Did Garrett know Savannah was dead? Had he been involved? Was he playing them all?

But... Elsie squinted at her screen. Something wasn't right. Some interference, a pixilation around the dog. Whatever footage that was, it had been tampered with.

"This isn't real," Elsie said.

"Sucks, huh? Your brother being a dirtbag. Rough."

"No. No, Mallory. This *footage* isn't real. Or isn't the whole story. It's been altered. I have to tell—" Before she could dart off, Mallory grabbed her arm and held her still.

"Wait, Els. Courtney can't know we're here. *Especially* if that footage is altered."

Elsie knew she was right, but the idea of Nate sitting there thinking Garrett had said all those awful things... It hurt. What's more... Mallory believing her when it was a crazy assertion—that the video they'd seen was altered to make things look a certain way... Nate didn't need any more disbelief in his life.

Mallory didn't question it. She trusted Elsie's expertise. Not only did Nate not have that, all these years he'd been trying to prove himself right, he now also had to believe his brother was actively working against him.

It wasn't fair, and Elsie needed to end that suffering for him as soon as possible. But Mallory didn't let her

arm go. As if she knew Elsie couldn't be trusted to follow reason because her feelings were *way* too involved.

Courtney packed up the laptop, gave Nate a kiss on
the cheek that had Elsie's hands curling into fists, and
then left the cabin.

They didn't have a camera on the dock yet, so she
had to sit and wait for Mallory to let her go.

"Mal, I want that laptop. Can you get it without
her knowing?" Elsie whispered, just in case Courtney
hadn't gone straight for the dock.

Mallory blew out a breath. "Eventually. But Shay
wants me here."

Elsie didn't say anything else until Mallory finally
let her go. A sign Courtney had to be rowing away by
this point.

"Connor says it's clear," Mallory said, tapping her
earpiece.

Elsie needed that footage. "Get it cleared with Shay
and get after her ASAP. I need that laptop."

Mallory nodded then peeled off in one direction,
already talking into the com unit. Elsie moved for the
cabin, watching the lake carefully to make sure Courtney was out of sight first.

She was a dot, far off near the other bank. So, Elsie
slid into the cabin without hesitation. "It isn't real," she
blurted even before she saw where Nate was.

He stood in the same spot he'd been when he'd told
Courtney to leave. Elsie thought she'd see anguish on
his face. Maybe banked fury in his gaze. But he nodded. Like he'd already figured that out.

Still, Elsie continued on, just in case he was being

stoic for the sake of it. "That video isn't real—not fully. If it were real, she'd let you have a copy. Or would have just sent you a copy, not come all this way. I saw some pixilation that…" Her technical explanations would take too long to detail—nor was he interested in them. "It's just proof that it's been modified. It was an altered video. Without the hard copy, I can't tell you what was real and what was changed, but if it was changed at all—"

"I'd believe a lot of things about Garrett, but being after my parents' estate isn't one of them. None of that made sense, so it makes just as much sense it's altered video."

"Well. Good." He believed her and in his brother and…good.

"They showed me that for a reason," Nate said, staring at the table Courtney had put her laptop on. "They want me to think Garrett is against me and Courtney isn't. But it has to be more than that. What do they care what I think?" Then he focused on her fully. "How did you know what was going on?"

Elsie went over to the phone hanging from the wall. She tapped the speaker. "I put a bug here." Then she pointed up at the light fixture, where she'd fastened a tiny camera that was as black as the fixture, making it hard to see if you weren't looking for it. "Video up there."

"You think of everything."

"Not everything," Elsie said, a slow, horrible realization taking hold. What did they care what he thought? That wasn't the important question.

"How did they know to include Savannah in this? And why send Courtney as messenger? It connects them. It connects both of them to whatever is going on."

"Maybe they think I'm too stupid to put that together."

Elsie shook her head. "If they thought you were stupid, they wouldn't work so hard to discredit you. They want you dead, but…they've had time to make that happen." There were too many contradictions. But there was one clear fact Elsie knew, and whatever happened because of it was all her fault.

"The problem is, if they know we made a connection to Courtney and Savannah, they know what I'm researching. They have to know or assume you know about Courtney and Savannah's connection."

"Or they're trying to get me to know. Maybe it supports this fake story about my parents' estate."

"Maybe." Too many twists and turns to see clearly. "I sent Mallory to get the laptop. That could help us answer some questions."

"How many more of these people are in your group?"

"Why?"

"I want someone on Garrett. And someone on my parents. I want…" Finally all that stoicism melted and his shoulders sagged. He sank into the seat at the table and rested his forehead on his palms. "Hell, I want this over."

Elsie swallowed at the tightness in her throat at all she wanted to tell him, to give him. She crossed to him, but she didn't know what to say.

He blew out a breath. "We need to get some rest.

I think I heard somewhere that you can't take down military groups who make no sense when you're exhausted." He got up and took her hand. She was so surprised by the move, she let herself be led into the back of the cabin where there was a bedroom. A *bedroom*.

"No funny business, Rogers," he said, walking with her into the tiny room.

She laughed and flipped on the light. The room was barely big enough for the twin bed that took up most of the floor space. She supposed it worked for whatever fishing weekend you might have, but it certainly wasn't going to fit two people.

"What about a little funny business?" she asked, looking up at him and hoping to take his mind off of all of this, if only for a moment.

She did get a half smile out of him. Then he looked at her that way he did that had all those fragile pieces of herself melding together until they almost felt stronger than anything that had come before. He pressed his lips to hers. A brief, gentle kiss.

It felt like a promise for something bigger than kisses or funny business. "Come on, Els. Let's sleep."

THEY DID IN fact sleep. She was dead on her feet before he'd even gotten her horizontal, and he wasn't far behind. He should have left her on the small twin bed and gone to sleep on the couch. But somehow he'd ended up tangled with her in the tiny bed. Sleeping.

Just sleeping.

There wasn't anything complicated about sleeping in the same bed as Elsie—he'd been dead to the world, after all—but, boy, was there something complicated about waking up with the woman. Elsie was all wrapped up around him, strands of her hair tickling his jaw, the steady rise and fall of her breathing making it next to impossible to move. His arm ached where he'd been shot, but he barely felt it when he looked at Elsie's sleeping face.

His life was wholly devoid of this type of thing. He lived on a ranch meant for rehabilitation, which meant he slept in bunks and was surrounded by men for the most part. Added to that, he kept to himself, focused on the mission of proving himself right or sane or *something*.

There wasn't a lot of softness in his life, and there never had been. But Elsie was soft, and lying with her felt like a kind of domestic comfort he'd never had or thought he'd wanted. It was strange to find contentment in it.

He couldn't dwell on that for long. He heard the faint squeak of a door being opened. No doubt Elsie's team already knew they'd crashed, but he doubted they knew he and Elsie had crashed together.

They certainly didn't need to draw any of the wrong conclusions.

Nate eased out of bed, carefully disentangling himself from Elsie. She murmured something then buried her face in the pillow and stilled.

Nate moved silently out of the bedroom.

Mallory was sitting on the couch, scrolling on a phone. She glanced up when he entered the room. "Could have slept longer. Looking a little rough there."

Nate grunted. "I was awake."

Elsie stumbled out of the room with a big, loud yawn. If Mallory thought anything of that, she kept it to herself.

"I've got the laptop," Mallory said to Elsie.

Elsie lurched forward. She said something, but it was mostly a mumbled garble.

"Coffee?" Nate asked, knowing Garrett would keep at least that in the kitchenette even if he hadn't stayed here in a while.

Elsie shook her head. "Does anyone have any pop?" She plopped herself at the little table.

Mallory put the laptop on the table and then went to the mini-fridge and pulled out a can of Coke. "I stocked up while you two got your beauty rest."

Elsie yawned and didn't tell her friend to go jump off the dock, so Nate figured she was a better morning person than he was.

"Do you subsist solely on sugar?" he muttered in Elsie's direction.

"If I can help it," Elsie replied. She was already studying the laptop, though she was looking at the outside, examining all the ports and jacks and whatnot. "You dusted for prints?"

Mallory nodded. "Collected what I could. It hadn't been wiped since her trip out here, but it might have been before that."

Elsie nodded then opened the laptop. She took a big gulp of pop, making Nate wince. But she got straight to work as if she was indeed powered solely by sugar. She frowned, tapped, leaned too close to the monitor.

"It looks like it's only got the video on here. Imported from somewhere else."

"So, it's a dead end?"

Elsie made a *pfft* sound. "With computers, nothing is a dead end." She looked up at Nate, eyes soft and full of all those tangled emotions he hadn't quite figured out. "But this is going to take some time. You should probably talk to Garrett about everything."

Nate winced. God, that was the last thing he wanted to do. He knew he had to, but that didn't make the prospect of actually doing it any easier.

"He's here," Mallory said.

Nate whirled to face her. "What?"

"Shay's orders." Mallory shrugged. "Once he got Don situated with the state, he started asking the kinds of questions we can't really have people asking, so Shay told me to pick him up."

"You kidnapped my brother?"

"I mean, I would have enjoyed that and all," Mallory said with a grin. When Nate did not return it, she sobered. "No. He came willingly." She nodded to the door. "I'll take you to him."

"Who's going to stay with Elsie?"

Elsie rolled eyes. "I might survive what with the three other operatives patrolling the island."

Nate didn't particularly like that answer, but Garrett was here and deserved some answers. So, Nate followed Mallory outside.

"We figured it's his cabin, so it wouldn't raise too much suspicion for him to be here. And Courtney knew you were here, so it could be a brotherly fishing trip."

"Unless they know you guys are also here."

Mallory shrugged, leading Nate into the wooded area at the far end of the island. "Maybe they do. Maybe they don't. We'll do our jobs either way."

"I still don't understand your 'job,'" Nate muttered, ducking under a low branch.

"To help. It's just that simple." Mallory stopped in a small clearing. Garrett was pacing the area, Shay was sitting next to a small campfire.

Both Shay and Garrett looked up. Garrett stopped pacing but Shay stood. "We'll give you guys some privacy." She nodded to Mallory and they disappeared into the trees.

"Somehow I doubt we're really getting privacy," Garrett said, scowling at the trees.

"Yeah, me too. Mallory said you were asking questions."

"Yeah, I've got questions. I think I've got this all figured out, then a million what-ifs pop up. Someone tried to *kill* you, Nate. Someone was hired to take you out."

"Yeah, turns out corrupt military leaders don't take kindly to the truth."

"This isn't a joke."

"No, I guess not."

"Someone wanted you dead. I want answers. I want to know how we're going to stop that from becoming a reality. I can't sit in my office twiddling my thumbs. Not when a hitman is after my brother."

Nate wished he could feel comforted by that. Wished he could tell his brother this had nothing to do with him and he could take a hike—just so Garrett would be out of harm's way. But…well, aside from the fact Garrett wouldn't take any hikes, no matter how much of a jerk Nate pretended to be, Garrett was involved. At least tangentially.

Nate didn't know how to say that to Garrett, except plain and quick. "I'd love to tell you I can handle it, but unfortunately you're more connected than you think. Savannah is wrapped up in this somehow."

Garrett's expression shuttered. Immediately. It had been like that this entire year since Savannah had left. One mention had him closing everyone off. He didn't rage. He didn't get upset. He shut down.

"Apparently she's Courtney's cousin. They share a grandfather who's a vice admiral in the Navy. Those facts alone wouldn't be that big of a deal but—"

"Connected to military conspiracies, it's not so far-fetched."

"Yeah, and Savannah left when…"

Garrett's expression slackened. "When you told me. You…" He stood there, looking like he'd been shot. He'd gone pale. He turned away from Nate, stalked toward the trees then back into the clearing.

"Garrett—"

"You told me, and I told her I thought it was worth mentioning to a higher-up. Maybe you weren't quite adjusting the way we'd hoped, but maybe there was some seed of the truth in it. You gave me those print-outs and…"

"And what?"

"They were gone when she left. I was dealing with

other things, so it never occurred to me to connect it. It never occurred to me…"

"You never told me you were going to send those printouts to anyone." That there'd been some small belief mixed in with all the worry over him.

Garrett shrugged. "You were certain."

Nate didn't have time to deal with the emotions battering him. Garrett deserved the whole truth. "There's more."

"How could there possibly be more?" Garrett rasped.

"Savannah…died."

"What?"

"In childbirth." Nate swallowed. "With twins. Who survived."

"You're telling me I have children out there…and I… Where?"

Nate didn't know how to deal with the ragged emotion on his brother's face, or the fact that it wasn't even that simple. "They might not be yours, Garrett. But they're with Savannah's grandparents."

"If they were someone else's, don't you think they would be with that someone else?"

"We don't know. We just don't know."

"She didn't…" Garrett stood there, and Nate knew his world view was crumbling bit by bit. Nate had been in the same situation too many times to count. Everything you thought you knew or understood upended. All the people you thought you could trust turned out to be someone else.

"Look, Garrett, we're still figuring this all out. It's confusing and complex, and yeah, someone wants me dead for it. You're connected, so I want you to stay safe, but you don't have to—"

"Elsie. She's tech. Computers and hacking, right? And this team she's with… They don't have to follow laws, so to speak."

"They're the good guys, Garrett. I'm sure of it." He wasn't sure of much else. But that, he'd come to believe.

"I don't care about that. I need to know if those kids are mine. We need to know…where this started, and why you. We need to stop this, whatever it is. Someone wanted you dead, Nate."

"I think it's more than some*one*."

Garrett clearly did not find his words comforting. "I took that guy to the station, booked him and got him sent off to state. But I'm sitting there, hands tied, while you're with this group. Someone wanted you dead, and I was playing small-town cop. Now—"

"We need you to play small-town cop."

"Not anymore. I'm part of this now. You. Savannah. Whatever it ends up being, I'm part of it."

"I know I joke about the crime in Blue Valley, but you're the only cop. You have to be there."

"Even the only cop has sick days. I'll call Valley County to send out a detachment the next two or three days. Mrs. Linley will dispatch all calls to them."

"You sure?"

"Someone wants my brother dead. My ex-wife is dead and maybe left my children with her crooked family. Yeah, I'm damn sure."

Chapter Seventeen

Elsie's head throbbed and her vision was blurry, but she was used to that. Working at a computer screen day in, day out took a weird physical toll some days. But the part she wasn't used to, the churning, awful part, was realizing she might be a computer genius...but she was hardly the only one.

When the door opened, Elsie looked up from her computer. Nate and Garrett walked in, looking grim and handsome. They didn't make her nervous anymore. She trusted them, knew they were good men. Good men who'd been drawn into this awful thing simply because Nate had once wanted to do the right thing.

Shay came in next. "You got an update, Elsie?"

Elsie tried to smile, though she knew it faltered. "Do you want the bad news or the really bad news?"

"What is it?" Shay insisted.

Elsie took a shaky inhale. She'd made mistakes before. There was no way to be perfect when it came to computers or hacking. But she'd never felt the weight of responsibility sit quite so heavily on her shoulders.

She'd never before felt quite so outmaneuvered. No one in this room was going to take any of her news well.

So, she had to be the calm one. The one who knew what she was doing, even in the face of her own failure. "They've been tracking me."

"What? How?" Shay demanded.

"I haven't figured out the technology of it yet. It's virtually unheard of—in fact, a lot of tech people think it's an urban legend. It's complicated but, bottom line, they have a program that can attach to the hack and follow that computer's movements. As far as I can tell, they can't get a location or an IP, but they can watch your computer moves."

"So, they don't know it's *you*."

"No, but it wouldn't be hard to figure out. Maybe if I'd stayed at headquarters, but my arrival in Blue Valley... Nate's subsequent leaving Revival... Honestly? That hitman could have been after me as much as he could have been after Nate."

Shay swore. Nate looked apoplectic. Elsie felt strangely calm. What else was there to feel? They were all alive and well, and Elsie had caught on before an ambush had happened.

"But wait." Shay held out an arm. "That hitman was after Nate before I sent you here."

"Not exactly. We don't know where that hitman was. He certainly wasn't *here*, even when the hitman after Connor was in Wyoming. Maybe he didn't have a target yet. Maybe he had another one first. But I can't find any evidence Nate was ever the target there."

"This is my fault," Shay muttered.

That made Elsie feel a bit like a useless child. But she smiled at Shay and kept her voice even. "Don't go mourning me yet. I'm still alive."

Shay glared at her. "I shouldn't have sent you."

"You said there was no other choice."

"I should have found one."

"I'm not dead. I'm not even hurt." She pointed at Nate's arm, because he had been. "I wouldn't have found this if I'd stayed. I wouldn't have figured it out if I didn't have *this* laptop. Besides, this is where we are. There's no room for should-have-beens. We have to deal with what is. Now, we can wait for them to show up—"

"Can someone clarify to me who this 'them' is?" Garrett said. He held himself still, much like Nate did. There were similarities in height and breadth of shoulders, dark hair and eyes. A lot of similarities. But they were two very different men.

Elsie exchanged a glance with Shay. Shay's imperceptible nod was the go-ahead to share what North Star knew.

"Connor took down Daria, right? He was stealing weapons from the military and selling them to a group—which our team took care of. Based on my research, I think we're dealing with either one guy or a small group of what I'd call idea men. Whoever set the whole thing into motion is removed enough, it's almost impossible to make a connection to the actual group doing wrong. That means all they have to do is start a new group—if they haven't already."

"Yet we know, thanks to Courtney and Savannah, one of these idea men has to be their grandfather," Nate said. "We wouldn't have known that if they hadn't showed some of their hand."

"But they've already existed in Blue Valley together, and no one's put it together until now," Garrett pointed out.

"Yes. Now. Before Courtney arrived, I put it together. Via the computer. That they're tracking. They know someone put together Savannah and Courtney *and* Vice Admiral Loren."

"Let's discuss Courtney for a second," Shay said. "Why is she putting herself in the middle of this? Why not take out Nate via explosives in the computer or something? She had sufficient chance."

"Why they haven't killed Nate is an interesting question. Because I have to believe they've had ample opportunity. They're tracking what I'm doing. That hitman? It makes more sense for me because I'm the one making connections. It made sense to go after Connor first because he's receiving evidence."

Nate swore under his breath.

"But listen. Everyone, think about this. For two years they haven't taken out Nate. He's dug into information and told people, but they haven't killed him. They've only worked to discredit him. To destroy his evidence. Presumably, they had someone marry his brother. Presumably, they had Courtney's brother installed at Revival. Why?"

Everyone was silent because there was no good answer to that question. But there was *an* answer.

"They think I have something," Nate murmured, his scowl deepening. "Something they need before they can kill me?"

"It isn't simple enough to just extract the information from you. There's more to it. They think you have something *big*." Elsie paused. She didn't want to believe Nate was still holding back, but he had before. Multiple times. "Do you?"

"Not that I'm aware of."

"Why not kidnap him, then?" Shay said. "Force him to give the information. Or hurt his family. Blackmail. Why not force the information out of him?"

"I'm not sure. But I think it has to do with Nate not being aware. They're waiting for him to do something. But we interfered. And still, the worst they did was send Courtney out here to try to convince Nate that Garrett was against him, setting him up all for their family money."

"The *worst* they did was send a hitman for you," Nate growled.

Elsie knew that everyone was frustrated, confused and irritable because of it. But these were the kinds of puzzles that made sense to her, even when they didn't.

"The important thing is, I didn't think this kind of tech they've got was possible. But it is. That means I can turn it around on them."

"You can?"

Elsie nodded. "With the right plant. We need something to happen. Something they'd want to look into—and then I could turn their trap around on them."

"Like what?"

"Courtney gave me the idea, actually. She acted like she was concerned Nate would hurt himself, even insinuated he might end his life. What if they thought he did?"

Nate found himself speechless. He'd been thrown a lot of curveballs, but faking his own suicide was pretty up there.

"Fake kill him ourselves?" Shay asked.

"They want something from him, and they're afraid to get close enough to get it. So—" Elsie shrugged "—we eliminate the threat. I think suicide makes the most sense, since that's what Courtney was getting at."

Nate didn't know what to say. Garrett rubbed his hands over his face and Shay stood stock-still, presumably absorbing the information and coming up with a plan.

Nate had no idea how he'd ended up here, with multiple people believing him, setting up traps to prove everything he'd believed alone for so long.

"They'd need to be sure," Elsie continued. "They'd have someone hacking into police reports, hospital records, maybe even death records. All I'd need to do is watch for it. From there, I can use their own tactics against them. I bet they've got a lot more to hide than we do."

"Won't they just find out it's a fake?" Shay asked.

"I could make the documents look real, but I think it's better if it's fake," Elsie returned. "They'll think we think we've pulled one over on them, but what we're really doing is setting a trap. We watch them, instead of them watching us. We make sense of it, and once we do, we can really stop them."

"I'm sorry. You can't put my parents through this. Or Revival. It isn't right. It isn't fair."

Elsie's gaze met his. "While I'd argue the ends justify

the means, we don't have to. We've got Blue Valley's sheriff right here." She pointed to Garrett. "We've got the tech expert who's going to fake the records." She gestured to herself. "We don't need to bring in anyone else to make it look real. We only need *them* to think it's real, and then do one search on one specific event, and then I've got them."

"You're sure?" Shay asked.

"Thanks to Courtney's computer, I'm positive."

"So, what do we do?" Garrett asked. He sounded tired, and everything about his expression and the bleak look in his eyes reminded Nate of when Savannah had first left. Garrett had been wrecked, and this was the same. If not worse.

Before he could help his brother through his turmoil, they had to end *this* thing.

"Does anyone know you're out here, Garrett?"

"When Mallory so insistently said I had to come with her, I told Mrs. Linley I had a meeting and to route dispatch through Valley County. I didn't say where the meeting was or who it was with."

"So, you'll call in a potential suicide and—"

"No, I can't lie to Mrs. Linley. Not about that. If I tell her where I am, she'll know. Besides, she'd have it spread around Blue Valley and Revival in five seconds flat."

"Okay. Well, what if you called her to say you were going to check on your brother at your cabin? She doesn't have to know the end result we're trying to create, and you'll be able to help me generate a fake report from here."

Garrett clearly didn't like it, but he nodded. "Okay. Then what?"

Elsie and Garrett hashed out the details of medical examiners and records. Of his fake death. Nate didn't have anything to add to all that. It was mostly just an out-of-body experience standing in the middle of his brother's fishing cabin while people *helped*.

But he didn't have time to be completely useless. He had to think over two years of events—even ones like Savannah leaving, which felt unrelated—and try to figure out why this group wanted *him* alive, but weren't going to press him for the information they needed.

He had no possible idea what they could think he had, but he supposed he should be grateful for whatever it was.

Garrett was leaning over Elsie's computer. "All this is how you figured out Savannah died?" Garrett asked Elsie, frowning at the screen.

Elsie looked at Nate briefly and then nodded at Garrett. "I promise you, when I can, I will use whatever is at my disposal to either get some kind of paternity check, or to prove that you have a right to one."

Garrett inhaled, but he shook his head. "First, we do this."

"Yeah. First we do this." She looked up at Nate and offered a smile. A clear attempt to lighten the mood. "Just a couple Blue Valley kids taking down military corruption. Who would have guessed?"

Chapter Eighteen

When Elsie looked up from her computer some time later, she was alone. Well, she doubted she was *alone*. Neither Shay nor Nate would leave her unsupervised, but the cabin was empty save her.

She rolled her shoulders and rubbed her eyes. She'd worked through the night, but that had been fine because she'd slept for half the day yesterday. She'd been totally unaware of people coming and going, so she had no idea if people were asleep, outside or what.

She'd done all the work to make it look like Nate had died. It was going to be a pain to undo, but she'd cross that bridge when she came to it.

For now, for all intents and purposes, Nate looked dead to someone who would look. Since she'd had Garrett call Courtney and ask her to come into his office today to make an official statement about her visit to the fishing cabin, she thought Vice Admiral Loren or someone he employed would start looking into that death soon.

If Courtney didn't spread the word to her grandfather, they'd have to come up with a new way to care-fully make sure he got the information.

Elsie got up and stretched. She needed a five-minute break from looking at the monitor, and then she'd get back to it. Waiting for *someone* to start looking into Nate's alleged death.

She looked out the window. Everyone was outside in the dim light of morning—Shay, Mallory, Gabriel, Connor, Nate *and* Garrett. It was the thing she'd always appreciated about being part of North Star. No matter how bad things got, they were a team. They worked together and fought together. All without coming unglued.

For a while there, Elsie had only known how to come unglued. North Star had saved her from that, and now here she was. In Blue Valley. With people who'd known her then and people who knew her now.

She hadn't fallen apart. She wouldn't. She had a job to do. She'd do it because North Star meant the world to her. She'd do it because…well, now so did Nate.

She sighed and watched as it looked like they were putting up targets for doing some sort of practice.

Guns and shooting. No thank you. Elsie would stay inside and keep to her computer work. She got herself a can of Coke and then settled back at the computer.

It didn't take much longer, and she got so absorbed in what she was doing, she didn't even hear the gun-shots outside. Someone was poking into things. Now, all she had to do was run her program.

She got lost in it, like she always did. Here, she was all powerful. She got everything she needed to use Courtney's computer to reverse the program that would now stalk their every move. She might even be able to hack into a computer or two—figure out who was behind it.

Her fingers flew over the keys and she ignored the crick in her neck.

"Jackpot," she muttered. Emails. Including one about a chartered plane. She jumped to her feet and hurried outside. They were still shooting, and Elsie tried not to let her distaste show as she crossed to Shay. Gabriel liked to give her a hard time for being squeamish about guns while working for a secretive group that used a *lot* of heavy artillery. She understood why North Star operatives or even police officers needed to practice this kind of thing, but there was nothing about the noise or the machines themselves that Elsie had ever found any comfort with.

Elsie kept her distance until Shay told them all to stand down.

"Come to show us how it's done?" Shay asked.

Nate eyed her skeptically. "*Can* she show us how it's done?" he asked, clearly not believing Elsie'd had any training. It was hard to blame him. She'd been a shaky mess when holding the gun earlier.

"She's a phenomenal shot," Shay said proudly. "When she's not nervous," she added.

"Really?" Nate clearly thought Shay was trying to pull one over on him.

Elsie lifted her chin. She was not going to be drawn into this banter. "I really prefer to *not* handle guns."

Before she could tell them all that they had more important things to concern themselves with, Nate moved to pass her his gun. "Show me."

She didn't take the gun, but there was something in his expression. Not disbelief exactly, but a kind of good-natured humor that was hard to resist. "Fine," she muttered and took the gun.

They'd hung debris from tree branches using fishing line, so that the targets fluttered and moved with the breeze. Elsie chose three pop cans, raised the gun and aimed. She nailed three cans in a row. She could have done more but she *really* didn't like guns.

She looked over at Nate. "Satisfied?"

Garrett let out a low whistle and Shay was chuckling. Nate was smiling, and it made that fragile thing flutter in her chest, which she was very afraid Shay would see right through. For some reason, the thought of tough, indestructible Shay potentially seeing what she felt for Nate embarrassed her.

"Now, can we focus on what's really important?" she said primly, carefully handing Nate his gun.

"What's that?" Shay asked.

"Loren chartered a private plane about an hour after Garrett called Courtney. He'll be landing in Bozeman in about three hours, barring any airplane difficulties."

THE CABIN WAS a hive of activity. Plans were tossed out, rejected, altered, rejected again. Nate stood in the middle of it all and felt a bit like a Navy SEAL again.

There was something comforting about the fact it didn't fit so well. Though he'd been discharged, he had no desire to go back. It eased something inside him he hadn't even known he'd worried about.

He might not know what came next when all this was over, but he knew he didn't want to go back into the military, even if he was cleared.

Cleared. He still didn't know how to wrap his mind around that, so he figured he should focus on the people around him. Who were trying to find a plan to get to the bottom of this. Once and for all.

"We'll want a full team at the airport," Shay was saying. "We can't get around that."

"And one of us has to lead the team," Gabriel pointed out. "Me or Mal or Shay."

"Granger could—"

"My family is in danger here. Especially with Justin at Revival. Keep Granger with my family," Elsie said firmly.

Shay nodded, and Nate was a bit surprised she didn't pull rank and tell Elsie how it was going to be. They weren't like any team he'd ever been part of. Shay was clearly the one who made the final decisions, but she listened. She considered. It didn't have to be her way or the highway.

"You don't need to babysit me," Elsie said, frowning at her computer. "You can all go."

"Nate can't," Garrett pointed out. "He's *dead*."

"So, I'll stay here and watch after Elsie."

"Garrett, too," Shay said, standing.

"I can—"

She shook her head. "You're the distraught brother,

and the fact of the matter is, we don't know what's going on. He's coming here, but why? I want pairs."

"Do I not count?" Elsie demanded.

"Not with your nose in a computer, you don't. You do your thing, Garrett and Nate will guard you so you can fully concentrate on *your* mission. I'll take Mallory with me to the airport. Gabriel and Connor will go keep an eye on Courtney. Surely, if Loren comes here, he's going to hook up with his granddaughter at some point."

The activity went full buzz as they hashed out details, plans, com units. Nate got lost in it all, until everyone was gone, and it was just him, Garrett and Elsie in the cabin.

Elsie was sitting cross-legged on a rickety chair, nose pressed to her screen. None of those light-blocking glasses, and it didn't look like she'd done anything but mainline pop.

"You should take a break. Eat something with substance."

Elsie gave him an eye roll. "I'm working."

Nate grumbled what he thought of that and then slammed around the kitchenette, fixing her some kind of lunch. There wasn't much to work with since Garrett didn't keep it stocked and everything had to be stored in canisters to keep the mice out. But there was some string cheese in the fridge that hadn't expired, and some trail mix in a container in the cabinet.

He put the plate on top of her keyboard. "Eat that."

She looked up from the screen and glared at him. "Do you have to be so bossy about it?"

"Do you have to be so ridiculous about taking care of yourself? You need a keeper."

"Oh, do I? Were you volunteering for the task or was it assigned to you?"

Garrett cleared his throat. Nate had fully forgotten about his brother's presence until that moment.

"I'll, uh, just…take a walk. Check things out," Garrett said and then backed out of the cabin. Quickly.

Nate looked at Elsie. Clearly, they weren't really arguing about food, and *clearly* it was absolutely the wrong time to argue about anything. "I shouldn't let him out there alone."

"No, you shouldn't," she agreed. Sitting there. Staring at him. The temper in her eyes had dulled into something else. "I've got work to do." She pointed to her computer.

Nate nodded. But he didn't move. They didn't have time for this, but it bubbled up inside him. Bigger and more confusing with every passing hour.

So, he kissed her. Because, no matter how little sense *that* made—or yelling at her about taking care of herself—it was the one thing he knew he wanted. The rest was a confusing jumble of noise. But Elsie's mouth on his? Arms wrapping around his neck?

Yeah, that was clear. "I don't know what this is," he murmured against her mouth, because at least that was honest. Even if it didn't help.

Elsie looked up at him from her seat at the table, wide-eyed, her arms still wrapped around his neck. "I don't, either."

"Well, as long as we're on the same page." He thought

about kissing her again, even in this awkward position, but she disentangled herself from him. And that was a surprise. She'd been the one who'd wanted to take it a step further earlier, or yesterday, or whenever that had been. Now she was getting out of her chair, putting space between them and looking at him with a wariness he didn't understand.

"Eventually, this will be over," she said, clasping her hands together. "And I'll go back to Nor—my group, and you'll go back to Revival."

She at least seemed disappointed about that, even if he would have preferred her *looking* for a way they could be together. But he was struck by a new thought before he could fully absorb the hurt of hers. "If this is really over, I won't need Revival anymore."

She swallowed and looked down at her feet. He didn't know why. Didn't know what she was feeling. But it didn't matter, did it? It wasn't his job to figure out *her* feelings. It was his job to figure out his own.

In a way, he'd learned an odd lesson when no one had believed him. He just had to do his own thing. Make his own plans. Follow what he thought to be right, no matter what.

Even when people didn't think you were crazy, that was the way you built a life. Sometimes it might be right to lie or to try to deal with someone else's feelings because you cared about them. Doing what was right didn't mean doing whatever you wanted.

Yet sometimes, it had to be…laying out what you wanted. No matter what a person thought or did with that information.

He took her by the chin so she had to look at him. He didn't know what he saw in her expression. Something like fear, which didn't fully make sense to him. Or maybe it did. Wasn't part of what was rolling around in his gut *fear*?

"I don't know what happens next for me, but I hope you can figure out a way to be a part of it."

Her eyes widened and she swallowed, but she didn't say anything. Not yes or no. And that was fine. She could think about it. They had time. Sort of.

He let go of her chin. "I'm going to go stick with Garrett. We'll keep the cabin in sight. Yell if you need anything or find anything."

She nodded, watching him go, clearly reeling. The kind of reeling a person needed to figure out on their own.

Garrett hadn't gone far. He was picking up the shells from their shooting endeavor this morning and dropping them into an old coffee can.

"Want some help?"

"Sure."

They worked in silence for a while, until Garrett paused and studied at him for a good minute. "Elsie Rogers, huh?"

Nate shrugged uncomfortably. "Guess so."

"Smart."

"Yeah, so?"

Garrett laughed. "That was a compliment. Man, you've got it bad."

"I don't know what I've got," Nate grumbled, hunching his shoulders. "She's got no plans to stick around here and I…" Blue Valley was home. After Revival seemed like a pipe dream, but he didn't want to leave. He didn't need to get out anymore, like he had as a teen.

He needed to stay.

"Dad could always use the help," Garrett said casually enough. But it struck Nate that his brother immediately realized he wouldn't need to stay at Revival any longer, as well.

"Yeah, maybe." But no matter how much closer to his future than he'd been a few days ago, there were still some answers to find before he could make those decisions.

They finished cleaning up then walked the length of shore that allowed them to keep the cabin in sight. Both searching the horizon for a threat. Something.

All was calm and quiet. Almost peaceful. As time stretched out, it was almost possible to believe peace might be an option.

But then Elsie darted out of the cabin, running toward them.

"What is it?" Nate demanded.

She came to a stop in front of them, breathing a little heavily. "It was a decoy. The man who got off the plane." She heaved in and out a breath. "It wasn't Vice Admiral Loren."

"You think he knows we know he's coming?" Garrett asked.

"I really don't know what to think. It might have just been a precaution. I didn't know until he was already in the air, so it's difficult to believe he somehow figured out I'd gotten into his computer system before they sent the decoy."

"He wasn't on that plane, but that doesn't mean he's not coming," Nate said, scanning the horizon again. "What's Shay's next step?"

"They're all heading for Courtney. They'll keep watch there until someone shows up."

Nate nodded. "Good."

Chapter Nineteen

Elsie didn't like the look Nate and Garrett exchanged, but she didn't like any of this. Down to Nate saying things like he hoped she'd be part of his life.

Life.

North Star might have saved her, but it had also been an opportunity to ignore all that *life* around her. Not constantly be there while her sisters built relationships and marriages and *lives*. Had kids and raised them. Elsie preferred to be proud of them…from a distance. See a glimpse of it then go far away and bury herself in a computer screen.

"What if he doesn't go for Courtney?" Garrett asked.

Elsie was reminded she had a *job* to do, not a personal crisis to deal with. "I have to get back and watch the computer movements. It might tell us something, but I want at least one of you guys to keep an eye on Mal's body cam so we see what happens as it happens."

They immediately followed her back to the cabin. She set up her computer for Nate and Garrett. "You'll be able to see what Mal sees, and hear most everything,"

Elsie explained. "If there's trouble, we'll deal with it." If she had to call Granger off her family...

She shook her head as she settled herself in front of her computer. She couldn't think about that. One step at a time. Surely Loren, if he was really coming, would head straight for Courtney. Nothing else made sense. Now Courtney had four people on her, so clearly North Star was in good position to deal with that.

"They're just watching Courtney and Don's place," Nate said, studying the screen in front of him and Garrett. "Not moving. Not talking."

"So Loren hasn't arrived yet."

"Presumably. Maybe he's not coming."

Maybe. Elsie dug into the charter plane reservation. It appeared to be for Loren, so it was clearly meant to be a decoy. That meant she had to find some other kind of travel information.

"She mentioned working for a group," Elsie mused, delving deeper into what she was beginning to believe was Loren's computer.

"She didn't care if we knew about the group. That's fishy, isn't it? Even if she was pretending to be blackmailed by them, she was acknowledging and clarifying their existence."

Elsie nodded, hit a few more keys. "Maybe she's going rogue from the group?"

"Yet she was still trying to turn me against Garrett."

Elsie tried to listen and work, but eventually she got caught up enough in what she was doing that she tuned Nate and Garrett out as they discussed Savannah and Courtney. She put all her tech people on Loren. The program he'd run to watch her, his emails, his bank records. The more eyes they had on this, the quicker they could find…something.

Elsie wasn't sure how much time had passed when she finally found something of interest, or if anything had happened on the monitor, but this could be a clue as to Loren's whereabouts. "I don't think Loren was in DC in the first place," Elsie announced.

"Where else would he be?" Nate asked.

"I found a credit card. It's not Loren's, but it's connected to the computer. I could figure it out for sure, but we don't have time. There's a hotel charge in Bozeman for the past week."

"That's before you came," Nate pointed out.

"But not before we got your name," Elsie returned, looking up from her computer. "We had a few days with your name before I got here."

"Your group telling tales out of turn?" Garrett said, his voice cool.

Elsie tried not to be offended, though it was hard. North Star wasn't dirty. It wasn't possible, considering she manned the computers, background checks and the like. "No. No, but… We got your name from another group. A group with their own agenda. It's possible someone on that side either purposefully let it slip or accidentally. I don't know their tech person's credentials."

"You sure it couldn't have come from your group?"

Elsie pulled her gaze away from the computer to look Nate straight in the eye. "Positive."

"Okay," he said with a nod. Believing her. Or at least trying to.

"Why wait? None of this waiting makes sense," Garrett said. "It's giving us time to understand everything. To protect Nate. I'm glad he's not more of a target before he's ready, but why?"

"I don't know if this answers anything, but there's another line one of my guys found when looking at bank records." It didn't all make sense, but she knew there was something there. She jotted notes as she went through what her subordinate had sent her. They'd followed a payment through its circuitous route to… "This all started when you were in Yemen, right?"

Nate nodded.

Elsie frowned at her computer. "Loren is paying someone in Yemen. Sums of money over the past two years. There isn't a great pattern, except it's a lot of money and it starts at Loren's personal bank account, then he hides it, and then the receiver hides it. But I can track it. Why would he be paying someone in Yemen? Repeatedly. For two years."

"Blackmail?" Garrett asked. "Someone there knows what he's doing and is demanding payment?"

"Could be," Nate agreed. "My civilian informant knew about Daria, sort of. I certainly wouldn't have gotten that far on Daria without him leading me to answers."

"This could be him, then."

Nate shook his head sadly. "Died in the explosion."

"Someone who knew him? Knew what he was doing? This kind of money screams blackmail." Elsie clicked on the email another tech agent had sent her and skimmed the information. "Or ransom."

"Ransom?"

"Loren has a recording on his computer. It's a garbled message, but the basic gist is 'we have your son.'"

"Who's Loren's son?"

Elsie switched gears. She'd looked at Loren's family and knew there was a son, but she'd been preoccupied with Courtney and Savannah. "Ewan Loren. Courtney's father." Elsie did a remedial search and it took no time to find... "He was reported missing from a military base in Yemen."

"When?"

Elsie pointed at the date.

"That's the day after I was injured," Nate said flatly.

"What does all that mean?" Garrett asked, clearly irritated with the way nothing seemed to add up.

He'd have to join the club. "I don't know."

NATE WAS STARTING to get a picture of what was happening. It wasn't fully clear. It didn't fully make sense. But there was something to this.

"What was he doing at a military base?" Nate asked carefully, trying to weave the disparate threads in his mind together. "You said Courtney's military connection beyond Justin was her grandfather."

"There aren't any military records for Ewan." Elsie tapped keys and frowned. "Nothing that I can find."

"Why was a civilian at the military base in Yemen?"

"To visit his father?"

"Loren wasn't there." Nate shook his head. "Daria was there."

"So, the son is part of it. Somehow. Working with

Daria. Then he's there, doing whatever, and you have a local civilian who knew about it. Maybe he's the reason someone took Ewan and has been extorting money out of Loren."

"It doesn't explain Nate's connection," Garrett insisted.

"I know," Elsie agreed. "But we keep finding as we dig. Maybe we'll find the connection. But we know there is one. There has to be one."

"If Loren is in Bozeman, he hasn't made a move for Courtney yet," Nate said. "At least, as long as we've been watching. Maybe you should send your team to the hotel."

"That's Shay's call, but I'll update her and suggest it."

Elsie picked up the com unit Shay had left her and spoke in low tones. Nate watched the video and Garrett watched out the cabin window.

Nate tried to make sense of what Elsie's tech team had found out. The civilian who'd basically exposed Daria to Nate had been killed in the explosion. Nate had assumed it was something set by the insurgent group they'd been trying to find, but what if...

What if Daria had known about the civilian informant, or had found out, and had had him killed. Maybe Nate was supposed to have been killed, as well.

But then, why not kill him anytime in the past two years? What was keeping Nate alive? All this time? While they actively worked to discredit him, push him into PSTD or mental illness or something.

"Shay's sending Gabriel and Connor to Bozeman. Mallory and Shay are staying on Courtney."

"We need to be looking out here, too," Nate said. "If Loren wasn't getting off that plane, if he knows more than we think he knows, we could be the target as easily as him connecting with Courtney."

Elsie nodded. "I'll transfer the body cam feeds to my tech people so we can focus on information and making sure no one shows up here."

"Good."

They rearranged. Garrett stationed at the window, watching the docks. Nate watched the side window. On the other side of the island, the rocks would prevent anyone from landing. This was the only access point to the island, and they could see the entire shoreline from the two windows.

There were other possibilities. Someone could parachute in. They could attempt to navigate the rocky shore on the other side. Military men with deep pockets were certainly capable of the equipment needed to do those things, but it would require so much work. And once again, Nate had to go back to the fact that they hadn't tried to kill him or to terrorize him.

Something was protecting him. God knew what.

Yet no matter how long he stood watch at the window, he couldn't work it out. No matter how many connections Elsie made… Maybe that was the takeaway here.

None of it mattered. Not really. The hows. The whys. Maybe it only mattered that they ended things one way or another. Elsie's group was working on it. He and Garrett were helping.

And someone was closing in on them. So maybe the only directive here was to survive.

"We've got company," Garrett said grimly.

"Already?" Elsie said, alarmed enough to look up from her computer.

Nate moved to the front window. "How many?" He looked over Garrett's shoulder and out the window.

"Two boats that I see. Two in each. Nobody I know."

Nate scanned the lake in front of them. He hadn't been able to see this end from his vantage point, but there were, in fact, two small boats. Motorboats, speedy and agile. But not silent.

"They don't care that we might know they're coming."

"If they think you're dead, maybe this is just a 'make sure he is' type thing," Elsie suggested.

"Possibly."

"We need a better vantage point." Garrett looked back at Nate. He didn't need to speak what he had in mind for Nate to understand.

"You think it'll hold the three of us?"

"Maybe. Maybe not. But if we can get one shooter up there, it's better than being sitting ducks in this cabin that can be surrounded."

Elsie grabbed his arm before he could tell her to get ready to hike. "You have to stay out of sight. They think you're dead. They wouldn't have time to prove otherwise yet."

Nate pulled himself out of her grasp then took her by the shoulders. "If they think *I'm* dead, I doubt they sent four men after me. That means they're likely here for *you* and what you can do with your computers. Now, come on."

She shook her head, gesturing helplessly at her computer. "I can't find the connections if I go with you."

"You can't find the connections if you're dead. We're running out of time."

Elsie blew out a breath then marched away from him. In a whirl of movement, she shoved the laptop into a backpack and slid her arms into straps. She took her gun and held it.

"You can't carry—"

"It's Courtney's laptop. I'll toss it in the lake if I have to. But I'm going to keep it with me for right now in case I have a chance to do more digging."

Nate looked at Garrett, who shrugged.

"Fine," he muttered. "Out the back." He pointed to the back door and Elsie and Garrett followed. "Once we're outside, don't say a word. You need attention, tap someone." He looked sternly at both of them. "Not a word. Not a noise."

Garrett nodded and Elsie saluted him. Like this was a joke. But he saw the way she gripped that gun till her knuckles were white—and she hated guns. Preferred her computer. Maybe she needed to lighten the mood.

"Garrett first. Then Elsie. Then me. Go."

They funneled out, a single-file line heading immediately for the cover of the trees. The four men in boats wouldn't be too far behind. Nate figured he'd have about a five- to ten-minute head start.

So, they had to book it.

The terrain was rough, the tree cover dense, but Garrett knew this island like the back of his hand. Nate hadn't spent much time here since he'd been a kid, but he and Garrett had spent days upon days out here back then, pretending to be frontiersman and such.

But this was more important. This could be life and death. They hiked in silence. Nate was impressed. Elsie tripped over a rock at one point and didn't make a peep even as he caught her from falling with a jarring jerk of the arm. She mouthed a thank-you instead and kept walking.

They finally got to the highest point of the island. Twenty some years ago, Nate and Garrett had worked all summer to build the tree house that still sat on the branches of an old, thick tree.

"It's a tree house," Elsie said, in an awed whisper, looking up at the structure in the leaves.

"Yeah. It is. You're up first."

Chapter Twenty

Elsie eyed the planks nailed to the tree that were allegedly supposed to hold her weight as she climbed the giant tree and into the rough-hewn house above. A *tree* house.

She looked over her shoulder at Nate and Garrett, standing there like twin sentries who certainly weren't going to let her chicken out.

She swallowed. It wasn't that she was afraid of heights so much as she was afraid of *falling*. But falling was better than getting captured or shot.

Probably.

She handed Nate her gun and then started climbing, and immediately felt Nate below her. Almost around her. Like he was closing her in. That should have been a claustrophobic feeling...but it very much wasn't.

"The adage is true," he said into her ear. "Don't look down."

"But when you say that to people, they want to look down," Elsie said, taking the next rung and very, very much wanting to look down. To see how far she'd come. Her eyes wandered, she couldn't help it.

She blew out a breath and scowled. They weren't even a few feet off the ground.

"Just climb," Nate ordered, though there was some amusement in his tone. "And when you make real progress, don't look down."

They climbed, and it wasn't so bad when it felt like if she did fall or stumble, Nate's strong body was right there to catch her.

She managed to reach the top and scramble onto the floor of the structure. She held herself very still, half expecting it to sway or to crumble.

But it didn't. It held her weight, and then Nate's and Garrett's, still feeling sturdy beneath her body. There were walls on three sides, seemingly drilled or nailed or roped to the thick tree branches, but one side was mostly open into the leafy tree branches.

Elsie tried to swallow her anxiety. She glanced up from her sprawled position on the floor, to see Nate and Garrett both standing there looking down at her, twin expressions of concern mixed with amusement.

She wanted to be offended by that, but they didn't have time. Garrett moved to the open side and began to hack away at branches with a pocketknife. Once he'd cut a bunch of them off, the vantage point to the shore was clear, without cutting so much away that they could be seen in return.

"What now?" Elsie asked, pushing herself up into a sitting position. She wasn't quite ready to stand in here yet. No matter how sturdy beneath her body, she knew how high they were and, surely, that was precarious.

"We watch what they do," Nate said. "I guess you

were right about bringing your computer. You can sit there and tap away while we watch."

"And if they start coming for us?" Elsie asked.

Nate and Garrett exchanged a look. "Let's take it one step at a time."

She did not trust that response, or that look, but she was sitting in a tree house. With two grown men. Watching for people with guns to come hunt them down.

Elsie looked around the small structure dubiously, but Nate and Garrett moved with sure feet and confidence the wood structure would hold.

Please.

She scooted into the corner of two of the walls, leaned against the wall gingerly, then pulled the computer out of her backpack. She set up her hot spot again and checked her messages from her team. She skimmed the information. There were new layers, but nothing groundbreaking or that fully explained any of this.

She went through the information again, looking for an angle they may have missed or glossed over. She let the work distract her from where she was and what was going on.

The nonmilitary son being taken was something. *Something.* And what exactly were the payments? Ransom? It had been two years. Why would a smart, capable, military commander keep paying someone if they weren't returning the son?

A message from one of her techs popped up.

Some money coming back over to US side. Connects to someone in Montana. Still narrowing down. Sharing screen with you.

Elsie immediately switched over to the screen. She followed the twists and turns, then started her own search. Through all sorts of computer programs meant to hide the money and its eventual endgame. Elsie dug and dug and dug, and then almost dropped the laptop.

Courtney.

But why would she be taking money from the group in Yemen? The group that allegedly had her father?

Elsie had to dig deeper, and fast, but Nate was swearing.

Elsie looked up. Both men were standing there, pointing to the shore in the distance.

"It's not random-looking. They're tracking us," Garrett said grimly. "Should be hard once they get in the trees, but they can see the direction we went from the cabin."

"Hard to track us, but not impossible for them to be led right here," Nate said, his voice matching Garrett's for grimness. "We'll go down. Elsie will stay here. We can each take two, don't you think?"

"You might be a little rusty," Garrett said.

"Yeah, and you might be a little old."

They grinned at each other and Elsie gaped at them. "What is wrong with you two?"

Nate chuckled and shook his head. "Brothers. Now." He pulled the gun she'd handed off to him so she could climb up, then crouched in front of her and held it out. "Stay put. Don't climb down, no matter what. If someone who isn't us or your group tries to climb up, shoot them."

Elsie looked at the gun. She didn't want to take it.

She didn't want them to go down there and start trying to fight off men. "I'll call Shay. She'll send everyone back and—"

"No time. You can certainly call for backup, but this has to be dealt with now. We can handle this, Elsie. Take the gun."

She did, though reluctantly. "I feel like I need to remind you my aim goes to hell when I'm nervous."

He took her by the chin, looked her right in the eye. "Then don't be nervous, Els. You're a hell of a shot, and we're all going to come out of this on the other side just fine."

It was a platitude at best. He couldn't guarantee that, but she nodded anyway. Because she knew he needed to think he'd given her some confidence, some surety.

So she pretended, because as he and Garrett climbed down, she was none of those things.

GARRETT HAD ONE pair of handcuffs. Nate found some rope that had once hung from a branch as a tire swing. It was frayed, but it might do the trick for a quick hold. He used his pocketknife to cut quick lengths of it and then handed a few to Garrett.

Garrett may have never been in the military, but he understood Nate's quick hand signals. From the base of the tree house, they spread out.

If the men coming had any tactical experience, they'd move forward in sets of two. One pair would follow whatever tracks they found and the other would be watching for signs of life.

Nate scanned the area for tracks himself. Or anything that might lead the men to Elsie. A few prints in the mud, a few broken twigs. Nothing too overt, but Nate didn't have any idea what kind of trackers these men were.

He wouldn't let anyone get to Elsie, no matter what it took. That meant he had to calm himself. Focus. Slow his raging heart so he could hear above its thundering beat. He took a moment to breathe, to center.

Then he inched forward, gun in hand. He moved silently, listening, watching. He kept an eye on Garrett. They were yards away from each other, each moving forward carefully.

Nate heard someone talking and stopped, moving behind a tree. When he couldn't make out the murmurings, he moved closer. Avoiding twigs and anything that would make noise with ease.

"Yeah. Okay. So what?" There was a pause. "You handle the computers. We'll handle the confrontation."

Nate could see the man now. He was on the phone. Nate didn't see anyone else around him, but the guy held a powerful sniper rifle with an impressive scope. As he talked on the phone, his grip on the gun loosened and his alertness to the world around him waned.

Nate filed away what he'd heard, but he couldn't think about or analyze the information right now. He had to take his moment and disarm him.

It was easy enough. The man had been so preoccupied with a phone call, he hadn't been listening for Nate's approach. A quick grapple and Nate used the rope he had to tie the guy's wrists and ankles.

"You won't stop all of us," the man growled, clearly

trying to get out of his bonds. Nate wasn't sure how long they'd hold, but he took the gun and the phone. He searched the man's pockets, narrowly avoided a head butt.

He looked right at the man. "Watch me."

Nate didn't frown, but he studied the man's face and knew something was…off. Maybe the guy was a good shot, and he was certainly dressed tactically, but he didn't hold himself like military or anyone skilled in tracking or combat. He was wrestling with the bonds in a way that would only tire him out.

Nate stepped away, dread skittering up his spine. Something was off, but he didn't have time to figure out what. He glanced back at the tree house, half a thought to send Garrett back there to keep watch—though the chances of his brother listening to him were slim. Still…

Nate heard the *snick* of a tree branch being stepped on. A total lack of tactical strategies. The phone call. The noise. Could be accidents, extenuating circumstances, but Nate didn't have the feeling he was dealing with trained assassins here.

So, who the hell *was* he dealing with?

Still, these men were armed. So, trained or not, Nate needed to disarm them. He moved around where the noise had come from. He made someone out through the heavy brush, and then advanced from behind. The man hadn't even turned before Nate had him on the ground, securing his wrists behind his back.

It wasn't even hard, and the quick ease of taking these men down had a cold ball of dread sitting in Nate's stomach. Still, he tied the man's wrists and then flipped him over so he could do the same to his ankles.

The guy had to be in his seventies. And, while he was in good physical shape, why would anyone send an older man to do a young man's job?

"Where is my son?" the old man demanded, wriggling against the bonds.

Nate blinked, fumbled, but quickly recovered and got the man's ankles tied tightly. It dawned on him, no matter how little sense it made, that this was Loren himself.

"Why do you think I have your son?"

"Why do you think you're alive?" the man said, wriggling like the other captive. Desperate to escape the bonds. He wouldn't escape. He'd be exhausted by the time he managed to get any sort of freedom.

Nate almost felt sorry for him.

Nate heard the approach of someone else and ignored Loren and the other guy for a moment as he readied for another attack. But it was Garrett who appeared.

"Handcuffed one and tied the other to him about ten yards north," Garrett said. He was breathing a little heavily, and his lip was bleeding. He looked at Nate's two conquests.

He frowned at the older one, clearly as confused as Nate had been by his age. "It's…Loren," Nate said, still trying to work out what the man had said. "He asked me where his son is."

Garrett's confusion matched Nate's. "Doing his own dirty work?"

"Thinking I have something to do with his son's disappearance." Nate immediately turned and scanned the woods around them. "Something is very wrong here."

Chapter Twenty-One

Elsie fretted. She couldn't help it, and for once she couldn't concentrate on her computer. How could she just sit here and do nothing?

She'd updated Shay. Shay was reticent to take someone off Courtney and Loren watch, and Elsie had insisted she not let Granger leave Revival. Shay had grumbled about it, but had eventually agreed to send Mallory.

Still, it would take some time, and Elsie didn't know how much time they had. She tried to meditate. Count backward from one hundred. She tried to lose herself in following the information her team was unearthing.

But she couldn't do it. She got to her feet and gingerly moved toward the open edge. She peered through the hole in the trees Garrett had made. She could see the cabin, the length of the shore, and the lake itself stretching out. Sunshine glinted off the water. It would have been downright beautiful if she wasn't scared to death of what was going on down on the ground.

She blew out a breath, ready to force herself to turn

away, when she caught a glimpse of something out there on the lake. A tiny dot, but moving closer. A boat.

It couldn't be Mallory yet—Elsie had just gotten off the phone with Shay five minutes ago. Was it reinforcements for the first four men? Nate and Garrett wouldn't know to expect more men and then they'd be captured and killed and...

Elsie took a deep breath and ordered herself to slow down. Nate was always saying one step at a time, and that's what she had to do. First, she had to understand who or what was in that boat.

She needed binoculars or something. She pulled out her phone. Surely she could find some kind of app. She muttered and cursed at how long it was taking, and then silently chided herself for making noise.

Once she got the app up and running, she pointed her phone at the boat. It had gotten closer, and the app allowed her to zoom in. The picture was still blurry, but she could make out two people. They were rowing. So, unlike the four men who'd come before with their noisy motorboats, these two wanted to be undetected.

If she had to guess based on size, shape and hair— a woman and a man. But if they were North Star, Elsie would be able to recognize them. It had to be more of the group Nate and Garrett had gone after.

Elsie forced herself to think. She could rush down and run after Nate and Garrett to warn them, but they were men with experience. A former Navy SEAL, a cop. They knew how to deal with this sort of thing, and Elsie running in with half-formed warnings wasn't going to help them any.

She had to know what they were dealing with. Her job was information, not action. She used the binocular app again. She still couldn't make out the faces, but she took a few pictures and then sent them to Courtney's computer.

It was more time, but she uploaded the picture into her team's systems with the instructions to make an ID. ASAP. Once they did, they'd spread the information to everyone, including Shay and the team in the field.

But she didn't know how she was going to get the information to Nate and Garrett. She'd figure it out. She would.

She resumed her watch. The boat was making slow progress, so she scanned the forest below. Could she find Garrett or Nate? Make out what they were doing? Give them some kind of sign from here?

She scanned and scanned. Sometimes she thought she caught movement, the flash of color, but the leaves were too thick to be sure. The only way she'd be able to see them was if they went past the cabin and onto the shoreline.

Her computer pinged and she went to look at what her techs had found out.

Clear match.

Elsie gasped at the information. All alone in the tree house, she *gasped*. Because she hadn't expected this twist, and she certainly didn't know what it meant.

The woman in the boat was Courtney. *Courtney*, whom North Star was supposed to be watching. The man with her was Justin Sherman, her half brother at Revival.

And they were armed.

Elsie stood abruptly, forgetting all her earlier trepidation about the sturdiness of the tree house. She hadn't told Garrett and Nate about Courtney getting money from the group in Yemen, because people had come and they'd gone off to take care of them and…

Stop. Focus, she commanded herself. She made herself breathe slowly, evenly. She couldn't be of help to anyone if she panicked.

You can be tactical, Elsie Rogers. You are a North Star operative, one way or another. Start acting like it.

She let her mind focus on that, repeat the words over and over. On her last mission, she had been drugged because she hadn't ever considered that someone might come after her. She'd believed in the safe cocoon of her computers and information.

Now, she knew better, and she'd use that knowledge to make the right choices. Nate and Garrett had to know Courtney was out there. It was imperative. Because this was bigger than just the potential for danger. Somehow, Courtney was the central answer to all of this confusion.

Elsie looked at the planks nailed to the tree branch and the long, *long* way to go to get to the ground.

"I will not be a coward," she muttered to herself. She tucked the gun, safety on, into the waistband of her pants and then began the long climb down. She bit her tongue to keep her limbs from shaking with fear—the pain a good distraction.

She kept her eyes on every plank as each foot reached for the one below, and then the next, slowly picking her way along even as her heartbeat echoed in her ears. She didn't look down, no matter how much the impulse plagued her. She would *not* look down until she hit solid ground. She let her feet lead the way.

But then one of the planks gave out, and her grip on the one above wasn't enough to keep her steady. She was air-bound, falling and—

"Oof." She landed on her butt, not a second or two later. Because, thankfully, she had been almost at the bottom. She sat there for a good few seconds catching her breath, the adrenaline buzzing through her.

She had not fallen to her death or injury. She was fine. Fine. And she had work to do.

She got up, dusted herself off and looked around. Nothing. No one. Everything was silent, and though her butt kind of hurt, she was uninjured. So, she moved into the woods, gun in hand, ready to find Nate and Garrett.

And get to the bottom of this once and for all.

NATE HAD HELPED Garrett move the two men he'd taken down to where Loren was. All four tied-up men were now in a small clearing where Nate and Garrett could keep their eyes on them. Just in case they escaped the rope bonds.

But these were not well-trained men. That's what struck Nate as the biggest issue. Who came en masse and untrained?

"You were supposed to be dead," Loren said, sneering at them. "If anything happens to my son, you can bet you will be."

Nate was tempted not to talk. After all, he didn't need to give anything away to this man. But maybe he'd find out more with the truth. "I've got nothing to do with your son. I didn't even know you existed until a few days ago."

"You're a liar," the man next to him said. "We have proof you're working with them. *Proof.*"

"Shut up," Loren muttered.

The way they spoke, in general and to each other, Nate had to assume the second man was related to Loren, as well. Not some band of experts. *Family.*

Garrett leaned in. He nodded toward the south. "More people coming."

"Elsie's group?"

"Doubt it. Too loud."

Nate paused and listened. Yeah, whoever was coming wasn't trying to sneak up on anyone. Both he and Nate aimed their guns at the direction the noise was coming from. But the new person showed absolutely no fear.

"Let's put the guns down, boys," Courtney Prokop—or Loren, or whatever—said. Courtney didn't have a weapon of any kind.

"Why would we do that?" Nate returned. "Two against one."

Courtney held up a hand. A gunshot exploded in the air and Garrett jerked back. Hard. Nate felt his whole body freeze as Garrett fell to the ground.

"Now, drop your gun, Nate, or I signal for a head shot for your brother."

Nate knelt to place his weapon on the ground. He looked at Garrett. Blood stained his shirt.

"Just my shoulder," Garrett gritted out.

Nate didn't say anything. Garrett might survive the gunshot, but not without medical attention. The clock was ticking. He had to get them out of this fast.

"What do you want, Courtney?"

"Justice," she said earnestly, like it was obvious. "My grandfather tried to *use* me for his dirty business deals. Didn't you?" she said, facing Loren now. "You thought you could pull one over on me. You thought Savannah and I were dumb because we were women. Well, we showed you."

"What are you talking about?" Loren rasped.

"*I'm* the one who convinced Dad to go to Yemen. *I'm* the one who told the civilian group what was happening. I orchestrated everything, Grandpa. Because you thought you could cut me out of the profit."

She turned to Nate, pointing at Loren. "My grandfather and father are the bad men here. They were stealing military weapons and selling them to the highest bidder."

Loren paled. "Courtney."

"You didn't think I knew? You thought you could send me on your little errands and I wouldn't *know*? I'm smarter than you. All of you. And I am the good person here. I'm doing what's right. Stopping bad men. Like my father. Like you."

"What about Garrett?" Nate asked. Garrett was pressing his hand to the wound to try to stop the bleeding, but the pressure was not enough. And Nate had no idea where Courtney's shooter was so there was no way to stop him. Yet.

"Garrett shouldn't have gotten involved. He certainly

shouldn't have gotten Savannah pregnant. That was his biggest mistake of all."

Garrett made a noise, but Nate didn't know if it was in pain or out of reaction to what Courtney said.

"We took care of that, though. Didn't we, Grandpa?"

"Where is my son?" Loren demanded. This time of Courtney.

"I made sure that little group in Yemen kept him alive. I mean, what a cash cow, right? You were so funny, giving us all that money and running all those sad attempts to find him. You're sad, Grandpa. And you thought you could use *me*." She laughed.

She was *unhinged*. That was all Nate could think. But he had to…he had to get Garrett out of here. Alive.

Elsie was his only chance. She had to have heard the gunshot. Hopefully she'd sent her group an SOS.

He just needed to keep Courtney's attention on him, so help could arrive. "How do *I* have anything to do with this?"

Courtney turned to him. Wide-eyed innocence. "Fate? Luck? Divine intervention? You name it. I gave the information to the civilians, and they chose you. They chose you. Daria tried to kill you, but he failed. So you became the perfect scapegoat. But to be a scapegoat, I needed you alive, so I made sure my friends in Yemen put that stipulation into the blackmail against Grandpa. Sent Savannah here to keep an eye on you, from afar. I just had to keep you alive. Had to keep an eye on that friend of yours, too. Gosh, he became a problem when you sent him that evidence. Really shouldn't have done that."

Nate couldn't afford to be knocked off his axis by that, but he was. It was just too many different blows. "He's just fine."

Courtney shrugged. "He didn't know anything, though, did he? And all he got was Daria." She waved a hand. "Who cares about that. I wanted the head honcho. The big guy." She turned to her grandfather. "Since he thought so little of me."

Loren just sat there, looking at Courtney like she was a stranger and ghost rolled into one.

Nate couldn't say he blamed the guy.

Courtney shook her head. "But I'm forgetting myself. At this point, Nate, you've outlived your usefulness. And your little friends got a little too close to the truth. I gave you the chance to take care of things yourself, but you didn't take it. Shame."

"You're going to kill me."

Her expression became outraged. "I am *not* a murderer. I am the innocent victim here!" She held up her hands. "I don't even have a gun. Or any weapon, for that matter, because *I'm* the good guy."

"Then you can't kill me."

"*I'm* not going to kill you, Nate." She smiled. "But that doesn't mean you aren't going to die. Just remember, it's your own fault. Not mine."

Chapter Twenty-Two

Elsie was sweating. Even though it wasn't hot at all. But as she moved through the trees, doing everything she could to control her body's reaction to stress and fear, she felt winded and sweaty.

But she persisted, moving as silently as possible in the woods and toward the open shoreline. If she didn't find Nate and Garrett on her way to shore, she would follow the tracks back into the woods and catch up with them that way. Maybe she'd even help surround someone. Or capture Courtney and Justin herself.

She knew it was crazy, but she thought maybe if she believed herself capable of North Star operative–level things, she'd actually be able to do whatever was needed.

Then, out of nowhere, a gunshot went off and Elsie narrowly swallowed the scream in her throat. She still made a sound, but it was little more than a gasp.

She held herself very still, looking around her without moving her body. She counted, carefully. When no one burst out of the trees, or shot at her, she turned in a slow circle. She held her gun at the ready, and did the nerve-racking thing of turning the safety off.

She had to be strong enough to defend herself if it came to that, and she had to be *herself* enough to think. To use the brain she'd developed to put the pieces together and get to the bottom of this mystery.

The gunshot had not been that far away. Not down on the shore, but near her. Had Nate or Garrett shot someone? Or the other way around?

She tamped down the spurt of panic. She was a North Star operative, and she would do her duty. She began to make her way toward where she thought the shot had come from.

Each step steadied her. She wasn't going to hide in the corner on her computer. She was going to act. Protect. Save.

If she ended up hurt like Sabrina, or worse, she'd have *done* something. Something important. Little Elsie Rogers, who'd been nothing more than a sad story in Blue Valley her whole childhood.

But she was a survivor. She would survive this, too.

She moved. She searched. And when she finally saw someone, it didn't fully make sense.

Justin Sherman was in a tree, spread out over a thick branch. Courtney's half brother held a sniper rifle, pointed at the world below.

He was somewhat obscured by branches and leaves, but Elsie could see him well enough to make out who he was.

She stepped silently behind a tree, then tried to position herself to see whatever Justin was aiming his rifle at. She couldn't see through the trees, not from her angle, but she could see little snippets of color. People.

He was pointing a gun at a group of people. A group of people who likely included Garrett and Nate. Even though the rifle was trained on them, Justin's gaze and hold was relaxed.

But something changed after a few minutes. He tensed. He lowered his eyes to the site of the rifle.

Elsie knew she had to act.

Don't be nervous. Obviously, telling yourself something didn't usually have the desired effect, but she heard the words in Nate's voice. Felt his belief in her. She pretended Justin's leg was a target. A pop can swinging in the breeze.

Nate was depending on her. Garrett was depending on her.

She aimed. She pulled the trigger.

And prayed.

THIS TIME, WHEN A gunshot went off, Nate didn't see anyone around them jerk or fall. Everyone in the clearing looked around at each other trying to determine who had been hit.

After a few seconds, everyone seemed to realize no one had been shot.

Courtney let out a groan of disgust. "That idiot missed!"

She only had one sniper. That was good news. And if a shot had gone off that hadn't hit anywhere near them after hitting Garrett… "Or 'that idiot' got caught," Nate pointed out.

Courtney's face… It reminded him a little bit of a witch melting. Her expression changed into a slow, dawning horror tinged by madness. That was when she reached behind her.

She'd claimed she had no weapon, that she was a good person because of it, but a person in this situation didn't reach behind them if they didn't have something there to reach for.

Nate lunged. He tackled her to the ground, but she'd pulled a gun out and was waving it wildly.

Nate ripped the gun out of her hand, held her in place beneath him by pinning her legs with his, and grabbed her flailing arms and shoved them between his leg and hers, as well. She was rendered mostly immobile, except for her head, which she thrashed back and forth in an attempt to wriggle herself free.

"Still think you're smarter than everyone else?" he asked.

She let out a primal scream, thrashing and wriggling with renewed vigor. But Nate held her as immobile as he could, holding the gun aloft just in case she got an arm free.

Someone tried to take it from his grasp and Nate looked up to see Garrett. Blood seeped from his wound, but he was on his two feet. He took the gun.

"You need to—"

"I'll manage," Garrett rasped, but he was downright gray and certainly unsteady on his feet.

"Sit."

"We've got to find the gunman."

"The gunman was clearly taken care of. As he's not currently shooting at us." Nate looked down at Courtney. "Let me guess. Justin?"

Courtney screamed curses at him, and didn't tire of thrashing.

"I definitely need some backup, though." He could hold her as long as he needed to, but he wouldn't be able to get her anywhere to have her arrested or taken care of or *whatever* without some help.

"We need to check on—"

Before he could say her name, Elsie appeared through the trees. She held a gun. Wide-eyed, she looked a little pale herself.

"Didn't I tell you to stay put?" Nate growled.

"You're very welcome for saving your life." She looked down at Courtney, not seeming the slightest bit surprised to see her. "I shot Justin."

"What?" Nate almost lost grip of Courtney, but re-applied pressure when she wriggled.

"He was in a tree, with a sniper rifle." Elsie looked up, pointed vaguely, then took in the sight around her. "He was shooting down below. I figured at you guys, so I… Before he could… I…." She was clearly in some kind of shock, but then she surged forward. "Garrett, you were shot."

"I'll live."

His teeth were chattering now. He looked awful.

But they were…alive. All of them. And Courtney and Loren had been taken care of, more or less, and… God, he wanted to get out of there. Get Garrett to a hospital. "Where is everyone?"

"I called Shay, but—"

"Right here," Shay interrupted, stepping through the trees, Mallory and Gabriel behind her. "When Elsie called us, we decided to go ahead and close in on Courtney. But it wasn't Courtney. It was some woman who claimed Courtney was paying her to house-sit. I pulled everyone, except Connor."

"We need Betty—ASAP," Elsie said.

"She's on her way. I sent Connor to get a helicopter. He'll rendezvous with Betty and be here soon." Shay surveyed Nate. "Allow us."

Nate transferred Courtney over to the trio. She screamed and raged, but they tied her up and Gabriel dragged her away.

"She told us everything," Nate said, still kneeling and not quite able to move yet. "Loren tried to use her for his little business, without telling her what was going on. But she figured it out. Started working with the Yemen group, got her father kidnapped, then convinced whoever got too close who wouldn't believe I was crazy that *I* was the one with the Yemen connections, and that I needed to stay alive or Loren's son would die."

Shay nodded. "Once we're all in better shape, we'll go over the details, but for now we'll take Loren into custody in partnership with our military group. They'll take care of the legal side of things."

"They might have a leak," Elsie pointed out. "Courtney knew a group was helping Nate."

"They're working on that. But for today? We stopped a multilevel military corruption scheme. For good."

The faint sound of helicopter blades chopping through the air met them, and Shay shaded her eyes at the horizon. "I've got backup along with our doctor. Betty's going to see what she can do about Garrett's injuries herself. We'd like to avoid a hospital if we can, but I promise you, if it's necessary, she'll get him to one."

"I want to be with him."

Shay nodded at Nate. "Of course."

"I'll be fine," Garrett said.

"I'm going with you," Nate insisted.

"Justin is alive," Elsie said. "I shot him in the leg and he fell out of the tree, but he's alive."

"On it," Mallory said. "Why don't you show me where?"

Elsie nodded, gave Nate one enigmatic look, then disappeared into the trees with Mallory.

Nate didn't know what to say or to feel. The only thing that mattered right now was getting Garrett medical attention.

Shay clapped him on the shoulder. "It's over, Nate. Might not feel like it yet. But you did it."

You did it.

He didn't know what to feel about that. His two-year-long nightmare was finally over. But his brother had been shot and Elsie was...

Accomplishing something sure didn't mean life could go back to normal, but now there was the chance at normal.

Time to figure out what he wanted his normal to be.

Epilogue

Elsie helped Mallory find Justin. North Star got the island cleaned up after Garrett and Nate were helicoptered out. Elsie wasn't sure what she was feeling, or what to do next, so when Shay told her to join her in the boat, then get in a Jeep on the other side, she did as she was told.

Shay began to drive, and though Elsie wondered where they were going, she didn't ask. She was too tired.

"Granger talked to your family," Shay said after a while.

Elsie straightened in her seat. "What?"

"There was some concern about Nate's welfare, and yours, so Granger talked to your sister and Nate's therapist at Revival. Assured them everything was fine and explained that Nate had actually been right all along."

Elsie could only stare at Shay's profile. "He told them Nate was right."

Shay nodded. "Proved it enough, everyone believed it. I think your sister believed it because you'd already told her, but everything is set at Revival. I'll take you back there after."

"After what?"

"Where do you really want to go right now?"

"I want to make sure Garrett's okay."

Shay gave her a quick glance and smile. "That's what I figured. I'm taking you to Garrett's house. That's where Betty's been working on him."

Elsie slumped in her seat again. "Well, good."

"Listen, Els. This was a lot."

Elsie forced a smile. Shay was worried about her. Because she'd basically been in the field, without being a field operative. "I'm okay, really."

"I know you are. But you earned yourself a vacation."

Elsie's brow furrowed. A vacation? A *break*? Shay didn't want her... "You need me," Elsie protested weakly.

"Yeah, we do. Whatever comes next, we're definitely going to need you. But you know the great thing about computers?"

"They aren't people?"

Shay laughed. "Elsie, you have a family here. You love your sisters. Isn't it time you let yourself have that?"

"You want me to quit?"

"I want you to stay here and enjoy that before we move on to the next assignment. And maybe I want you to consider working remotely. Sure, you'd have to come into headquarters sometimes. But you could also do a large portion of your work from Blue Valley, with your family."

Elsie looked forward. She didn't know what to say. She'd never thought about living in Blue Valley before.

"Elsie, I never fully understood… I knew you had sisters here, of course, but I didn't realize you actually *liked* them." Shay shook her head. "You have family you love, who loves you. You should be *with* them. And I don't want to lose you at all, but I want what's right for you. You're part of my family, Els."

Elsie swallowed at the lump that formed in her throat. Shay hated displays of emotion, but she was giving one and…

"This isn't about Nate," Shay continued. "It's about your family. But… You're young. You have your whole life ahead of you. Burying yourself in your computer was fine for a while, but there's a big world out there. You shouldn't limit yourself. You should stay here for your family, if it'd make you happy, but I can't deny the Nate factor. If you like him…why not go for it?"

"Where is this coming from? You were mad when Reece and Holden left for women."

"I'm not asking you to leave. Certainly not for any man. I'm asking you to build a life. Believe it or not, mad as I was, mad as I *am*, Reece had it right. We all deserve to build a life at some point. You're not in the field. You're not putting anyone in danger. You could do everything I depend on you for here. Enjoy your family. Start something with Nate—hell, maybe eventually end something with Nate. Or maybe it works out. I don't know, but you deserve the *chance* at all those things."

"What about you?"

"What about me?"

"Don't you deserve a chance at all those things?"

Shay hunched her shoulders a bit. "Too late for me. Now, look, we're here." She pointed to a house on a pretty stretch of land, the mountains big and imposing in the background. Blue Valley, Montana.

Even when it had been her prison, it had been her home. And now…did she really want to come back?

"Go. Check on Garrett. Talk to Nate. I'm *requiring* you to take a weeklong vacation here. After that? You get to decide."

Elsie looked at Shay. She had no words. Only feelings. So she did something she knew her boss would hate, but she couldn't quite stop herself. She reached over and gave Shay a hug. "You're my family, too."

Shay stiffened, but she didn't let Elsie go. They held on to each other, the years they'd worked together, gotten to know each other, had each other's backs… It didn't need repeating.

They were family. Sometimes a hug was enough.

Shay pulled back, eyes suspiciously bright. "Go check on your friend," she muttered, waving Elsie away.

Elsie got out of the car and walked up the little sidewalk that led to the door. The house looked like it had been cheerful once, but had been ignored for a while, so it was a little sad around the edges.

Elsie knocked, and it was Nate who answered. Tall and broad. She remembered distinctly when she'd seen him on her drive up to Revival. Had that just been a few days ago? He'd made her nervous and now…

He pulled her into a fierce hug and she wrapped her arms around him, pressing her face into his shoulder.

Everything that had been coiled too tightly inside her relaxed.

"Hi," she murmured into his shirt. "How's Garrett?"

"Good. Betty said it was a clean shot. Take a while to heal, but she sewed him up. She said she already had a line on getting a paternity test for his kids, though Courtney pretty much verified that in her rant."

He didn't let her go, and she didn't try to move.

It felt right here. Nate felt right. Did the bad memories of Blue Valley really matter when she had good memories with her sisters, building their families? When she'd met a man as good and amazing as Nate?"

"Betty's great. She'll take good care of him, and we'll do everything we can to get Garrett to his kids."

"Why would you guys…?"

Elsie pulled back a little. "Garrett was hurt because he got mixed up with our mess. My group will do *everything* to make it all right. No matter how long it takes." She met Nate's dark gaze. There were so many words in her head, but she couldn't seem to put them in any discernible order.

So she simply got up on her toes and kissed him.

NATE KISSED ELSIE back with all his relief, all this *emotion*.

A throat cleared behind him and Nate belatedly remembered the presence of Betty, a doctor from Elsie's little group.

"Garrett's asleep," Betty said. "I'll keep an eye on him. Why don't you two go for a walk or something?" Betty gave Elsie a wink.

Elsie blushed and Nate realized…he got to do things

like this now. Take a walk with a pretty woman because he wanted to and he liked her. No threats. No worries about who believed him.

Just life.

He moved outside and closed the door behind him. The sunrise rioted around them when Nate had figured it was still nighttime. His days and nights were off but... It was all over. Things were going to go back to normal.

Whatever that was.

"I talked to Monica. My therapist," he said, not sure why he needed to tell someone. Out loud. Explain... what had changed inside him.

"Shay said one of our guys explained everything to her."

Nate nodded. "She apologized for not believing me... She also told me in the beginning she tried to verify my story. It was just that nothing matched. I realized... people didn't even automatically not believe me—even Garrett. Courtney and maybe Loren were working to discredit me and I..." She slid her hand into his.

Elsie's hand. And it felt right to walk hand in hand with her. Here.

He wouldn't wish what had happened to him on anybody, but it had turned out...pretty okay.

Revival wasn't the place for him anymore. He wasn't sure what place was, but walking around Garrett's yard with Elsie felt good enough.

"I can't be mad or bitter at anyone. Except Courtney and Loren and Daria and the rest. But not anyone in my life." His life. His *life*. He got to build his now. "So, what happens now?" he asked.

"My group will work with the government to facilitate all the legal channels to bring Loren, Courtney, Justin and all of those involved to trial in a court of law. We'll keep an eye on it and watch for corruption, and step in if need be, but usually these things go smoothly."

"Yeah, Betty ran me through all *that*. I meant for you."

"Oh. Well." She looked at the mountains, a strange frown on her face. "Shay wants me to take a vacation. Here. Visit my family and all that."

"Good, you could use one."

She looked up at him, studying him. Clearly looking for some answer he wished he had for her. She stopped walking, so he did, too.

"Then she wants me to stay here. Work remotely from Blue Valley. She said I had a family I loved, and I should be with them more."

Nate's heart tripped in its beat, but he didn't let it show. He didn't know *how* to let it show. He wanted Elsie here. He wanted that *after* he hadn't known how to dream about.

But more than all the things he wanted, he needed her to be happy. To make the choice that was best for her. He had to clear his throat to speak. "Oh, yeah? What do you think about that?"

She looked at the world around them again. "I never thought about coming back to Blue Valley permanently."

He followed the path of her eyes. Mountains and the town of his youth. "Me neither."

Her gaze met his again. "Are you going to stay?"

He nodded. "I figured out sometime during all of this that Blue Valley is where I belong. Not sure exactly how that'll work. For now, I think I'll help at my parents' ranch while I think about what I want to do."

Elsie swallowed. "I think I want to stay, too."

His mouth curved, no matter how he tried to pretend he was indifferent. That she could do whatever she wanted and if it was right for her, he would be happy for her and support her.

But he wanted her here. He took her other hand in his. "Good."

She laughed then shook her head. "Yeah, I guess it is. I'll get to spend time with my sisters. See my nieces and nephews grow up. And there's this really cute cowboy I think might ask me out."

Nate laughed. Outright. He couldn't remember the last time he'd done that. And now...*now* he'd get to do it whenever he wanted. He vowed then and there, to do it often.

"You better be talking about me."

Elsie shrugged, but she was grinning and when he pulled her to him. She molded to his body like she belonged.

Like they did.

So, he kissed her. A promise. A bright chance at a future. Here in Blue Valley, where they'd once been victims but now got to be survivors. *Thrivers.*

Together.

* * * * *

COMING NEXT MONTH FROM

HARLEQUIN

INTRIGUE

#2049 MURDER ON PRESCOTT MOUNTAIN
A Tennessee Cold Case Story by Lena Diaz
Former soldier Grayson Prescott started his cold case firm to bring murderers to justice—specifically the one who destroyed his life. When his obsession intersects with Detective Willow McCray's serial killer investigation, they join forces to stop the mounting danger. Catching the River Road rapist will save the victims...but will it save their future together?

#2050 CONSPIRACY IN THE ROCKIES
Eagle Mountain: Search for Suspects • by Cindi Myers
The grisly death of a prominent rancher stuns a Colorado community and plunges Deputy Chris Delray into a murder investigation. He teams up with Willow Russell, the victim's fiery daughter, to discover her father's enemies. But when Willow becomes a target, Chris suspects her conspiracy theory might be right—and larger than they ever imagined...

#2051 GRAVE DANGER
Defenders of Battle Mountain • by Nichole Severn
When a young woman is discovered buried alive, Colorado ME Dr. Chloe Pascale knows that the relentless serial killer she barely escaped has found her. To stop him, she must trust police chief Weston Ford with her darkest secrets. But getting too close is putting their guarded hearts at risk—and leading into an inescapable trap...

#2052 AN OPERATIVE'S LAST STAND
Fugitive Heroes: Topaz Unit • by Juno Rushdan
Barely escaping CIA mercenaries, ex-agent Hunter Wright is after the person who targeted his ops team, Topaz, for treason. Deputy director Kelly Russell is convinced Hunter went rogue. But now she's his only shot at getting the answers they need. Can they trust each other enough to save Topaz—and each other?

#2053 JOHN DOE COLD CASE
A Procedural Crime Story • by Amanda Stevens
The discovery of skeletal remains in a Florida cavern sends cold case detective Eve Jareau on a collision course with her past. Concealing the truth from her boss, police chief Nash Bowden, becomes impossible when the killer, hell-bent on keeping decades-old family secrets hidden, is lying in wait...to bury Eve and Nash alive.

#2054 RESOLUTE JUSTICE
by Leslie Marshman
Between hunting human traffickers and solving her father's murder, Sheriff Cassie Reed has her hands full. So finding charming PI Tyler Bishop's runaway missing niece isn't a priority—especially when he won't stop breaking the rules. But when a leak in her department brings Cassie under suspicion, joining forces with the tantalizing rebel is her only option.

YOU CAN FIND MORE INFORMATION ON UPCOMING HARLEQUIN TITLES, FREE EXCERPTS AND MORE AT HARLEQUIN.COM.

HICNM0122A

Three months ago...
When I'm done, you're going to beg me for the pain.

Chloe Pascale struggled to open her eyes. She blinked against the brightness of the sky. Trees. Snow. Cold. Her head pounded in rhythm to her racing heartbeat. Shuffling reached her ears as her last memories lightninged across her mind like a half-remembered dream. She'd gone out for a run on the trail near her house. Then... Fear clawed at her insides, her hands curling into fists. He'd come out of the woods. He'd... She licked her lips, her mouth dry. He'd drugged her, but with what and how many milliliters, she wasn't sure. The haze of unconsciousness slipped from her mind, and a new terrifying reality forced her from ignorance. "Where am I?"

Dead leaves crunched off to her left. Her attacker's dark outline shifted in her peripheral vision. Black ski mask. Lean build. Tall. Well over six feet. Unfamiliar voice. Black jeans. His knees popped as he crouched beside her, the long shovel in his left hand digging into the soil near her head. The tip of the tool was coated in mud. Reaching a gloved hand toward her, he stroked the left side of her jawline, ear to chin, and a shiver chased down her spine against her wishes. "Don't worry, Dr. Miles. It'll be all over soon."

His voice… It sounded…off. Disguised?

"How do you know my name? What do you want?" She blinked to clear her head. The injection site at the base of her neck itched, then burned, and she brought her hands up to assess the damage. Ropes encircled her wrists, and she lifted her head from the ground. Her ankles had been bound, too. She pulled against the strands, but she couldn't break through. Then, almost as though demanding her attention, she caught sight of the refrigerator. Old. Light blue. Something out of the '50s with curves and heavy steel doors.

"I know everything about you, Chloe. Can I call you Chloe?" he asked. "I know where you live. I know where you work. I know your running route and how many hours you spend at the clinic. You really should change up your routine. Who knows who could be out there watching you? As for what I want, well, I'm going to let you figure that part out once you're inside."

Pressure built in her chest. She dug her heels into the ground, but the soil only gave way. No. No, no, no, no. This wasn't happening. Not to her. Darkness closed in around the edges of her vision, her breath coming in short bursts. Pulling at the ropes again, she locked her jaw against the scream working up her throat. She wasn't going in that refrigerator like the other victim she'd heard about on the news. Dr. Roberta Ellis. Buried alive, killed by asphyxiation. Tears burned in her eyes as he straightened and turned his back to her to finish the work he'd started with the shovel.

Don't miss
Grave Danger *by Nichole Severn,*
available February 2022 wherever
Harlequin books and ebooks are sold.

Harlequin.com

"Sawyer?" Her voice sounded hoarse. She sat back on
her heels and looked behind her. He was a fair distance
away, moving more slowly than she'd have thought.
Ashley shoved to her feet, her knees wobbling as she
stepped back into the water and shouted for him. "You're
almost there! Come on!" But he was gasping for air, and
for a horrifying moment, he sank out of sight.

Panic seized her. It was pitch-black. Not even the moon
cast light on this side of the shore. No homes nearby, no
lights or guideposts. How would she ever find him?

But she would. He would not leave her like this. She
would not lose him. Not now. She waded into the water,
stumbled, nearly fell face-first, just as he surfaced. He
took a moment to wretch, his hand clutching his side as
he slowly moved toward her, water cascading from the
bag on his hip.

"What is it?" She'd seen enough injuries to know something was seriously wrong. She wedged herself under his arm and helped him walk the rest of the way to dry land. "Where are you hurt?"

"Doesn't matter," he wheezed as he dropped to the ground. He leaned back, still pressing a hand to his side. Blood soaked through his shirt and onto his fingers. "I'll be fine in a minute. We need to get moving."

She dragged his shirt up, tried to examine the wound. "I can't see anything other than blood."

"I know." He covered her hand with his, squeezed her fingers. "Ashley, listen to me. Valeri left with Mouse and Olena, but he ordered Taras and Javi to stay behind. They're coming after me, Ashley."

"Us. They're coming after us. Let me—"

"No. It's me they want. Which means you're in even more danger than you were before. You need to go on alone. Now. While it's still dark."

"I'm not leaving you." She slung his arm over her shoulders and, with enough effort that her feet sank into the dirt, helped him up. He let out a sound that told her he was trying not to show how hurt he really was.

"You have to."

"Hey." She gave him a hard squeeze. "You aren't in any condition to argue with me. I am not leaving you, Sawyer Paxton. So be quiet and let's move."

Don't miss
Prison Break Hostage *by Anna J. Stewart,*
available February 2022 wherever
Harlequin Romantic Suspense
books and ebooks are sold.

Harlequin.com